Cir(

Trisha McClanahan

This is my circus. These are my monkeys.

For my mother, who gave me the love of books and so much

more.

And Aunt Debbie, my lighthouse for this project.

NIKKI

It's Monday and my iPhone alarm didn't go off. It seems implausible, but it happens. Okay, maybe I didn't set it. But I think I did. I blame what happens from there on Apple. Really. Not user error but the damn phone itself. That alarm mishap starts it all.

The tension in my back is distracting. The stress of the week ahead, plus the race of trying to pull myself together and get out the door, makes me think that just this once it will be okay to start my day with a Xanax. Not even a full one, just a half or less. Enough to relax into the week instead of diving into it headfirst.

I rummage through my medicine cabinet and find the small bottle with Spanish writing. Only four left. I break a tablet in two and swish back half with the remains of last night's Diet Coke. I push the empty soda can into my already-full trash bin, forcing the lid closed.

I stumble around my two-bedroom Mar Vista starter condo, stepping over clothes and empty shopping bags, weekend residue I swore I'd sort before Monday morning, but here I am again.

I pull out of my community garage in my crossover, the car equivalent of CrossFit shoes—not as glitzy and showy as running shoes or as gas consuming as hiking boots. My microscopic version of an SUV has no pickup unless I gun it. To avoid the late-morning traffic rush, I swerve down side roads to take a shortcut to my office.

That's when I tap her.

Tap her, I swear! What is this middle-aged woman doing on that bike anyway? I barely nick her back tire, and she snaps around and flips me off. She yells words I can't hear. So I gun it. A reflex. A snap decision. And a thud.

I can't take my foot off the gas or my eyes off the road. I can't bring myself to look in the rearview mirror. I grip the wheel tighter and finally slam on the brakes about a block away. Maybe it isn't even a block. I get out and look at the grill of my truck-car and see dented metal and maybe some kind of spandex fabric. It still doesn't register really, and as the Xanax starts to kick in, I remove myself from the scene entirely. I am still standing there looking at my fucked-up car, but in my head, I'm thinking about the quickest route to work. *How late am I going to be?*

A car behind me starts honking, then pulls around my car and me. He either doesn't see the downed cyclist or chooses not to get involved. Some wound-up jackass in a poor man's sports car. He could use a Xanax too. I later found out he did get involved, if calling 911 without stopping is considered "getting involved."

I stand there in the street, not sure what to do next, but I'm forced to decide pretty quickly. I hear sirens. I get back in my car to turn around to go back to the old lady. I promise, that's my plan.

But before I can drive the block—half block—to get back to her, more sirens. Cops on foot in front of me and in my side mirrors. Even then, I'm slow to stop. *I just need to circle around and get back to where she fell off her bike* I later find out that not stopping is called "leaving the scene of an accident" and "evading arrest."

Once I stop, one of the cops, a tiny woman who points a gun right at me, RIGHT at me, opens the door and demands I get out of the car. I do. But that isn't enough for her. She grabs my wrist and jerks it behind my back. I can feel the butt of her gun as she gropes my body, searching me for God knows what. She jerks my other wrist behind me and snaps on handcuffs. For a small woman, Tiny is very strong.

This isn't my first time in handcuffs. But the other times were all fun and games and in a bedroom, if you know what I mean. This shit is real. And it hurts.

The tiny cop reads me my rights, just like on TV, while the male cops huddle around us. It's a movie, except it is happening to me. Cliché but real.

Over Tiny's shoulder, I see paramedics at work on the female Lance Armstrong. One of her legs is bent strangely, in a way I didn't know legs could bend, and the EMTs are scooting a hard stretcher under her, like sliding a note under a door. The woman's eyes are open, but she isn't making any sound. If she is, I can't hear it over this cop's ongoing monologue.

When Tiny is done, she grabs my elbow and pulls me toward a cop car.

"My purse! My car!" I say.

She ignores me and continues to drag me toward the open back passenger door of her police sedan. She puts her hand on top of my head as I lower myself to get in the car, but I bang it anyway. I've seen this scenario in every police drama ever. It turns out it's actually real.

"Do you understand what I said to you?" Tiny asks. "Have you been drinking this morning?"

"Drinking? I'm on my way to work!" I reply with maybe slightly too much bitchiness given the situation I'm in.

"Did you take something?" Tiny says as she leans down into the open door, looking at me.

"Of course not!" And I mean it.

It's only later, as Tiny drives me away from the scene, away from the strangely bent leg of the bike rider and my not-a-car-but-not-a-truck SUV, that I remember the Xanax. But that doesn't count. Right? I don't feel like leaning forward from the back seat to speak through the wire-covered glass partition, which is the only way to disseminate this information to Tiny.

By the time we pull into the police station, whatever relaxation the Xanax had given me has worn off. First, I have to figure out how to get out of the back seat of the cruiser. Try getting out of a car with your hands tied behind your back sometime. Tiny helps pull me out, and I stumble. I stutter-step before I regain my balance. *Now she probably really thinks I'm on something.* Plus, I'm wearing wedges and a skirt. You know that saying about how Ginger Rogers did everything Fred Astaire did—"but backwards and in high heels"?

It's true about getting out of a cop car as well. The whole thing is set up for men. Or at least someone not wearing a skirt.

You know all those mug shots of celebrities or criminals where they look out of their gourd? I get it now. The photo is taken with blaring lights shining in your face, and it's super quick. They could at least give you a countdown like the DMV. Or have better lighting. No wonder everyone always looks fried in those pics. That's why mine looks like I am a lunatic, not because I'm on anything.

One thing I'll say—it's not like I'm asked to strip and then put in a paddy wagon to the state prison. I have visions of *Orange Is the New Black* and assume some lesbian encounter is waiting for me, but I'm put in a holding cell, still wearing my own clothes. It's a group room with two long benches and what smells like a couple of homeless women already in there. A lone exposed toilet is attached to a wall in the corner. *Note to self: no water until I'm out of this room.*

"You guys come here often?" I say to my cellmates.

"Fuck off!" one says to me. The other one laughs and spits in my direction. Gratefully, the loogie lands on the floor at my feet instead of on me. I gag a little but try to hide my disgust. I need to fit in with my new companions.

My wrists ache where the cuffs were. I've always been allergic to cheap jewelry, anything with nickel in it. I'm getting that itchy feeling already from those damn things. I wonder if they're available in sterling for sufferers like me.

***

"So that's the whole story," I explain to my lawyer.

Well, I *say* he's my lawyer. I'm hoping he'll agree to be my lawyer. I've only met him once, at a Christmas party where I may or may not have had too much to drink. He was on a date with a girl I think I went to college with—with whom I went to college, I mean. He's the only defense attorney I've ever met, and his name stuck with me. I gave it to Tiny earlier, and she dialed his office for me.

Mr. Lawyer ignores my concerns about the metal content of the handcuffs.

"Xanax? Why do you have a prescription for that?" he asks. We're sitting in a little alcove waiting for me to be processed, which up until this time I thought was something that happened only to cheese and convenience store food.

"What makes you think I have a prescription?" I answer. Sometimes my mouth is quicker than my brain. Turns out, this is not the kind of thing he finds funny.

As my brain catches up, I say, "My dentist prescribed it to help me sleep without grinding my teeth." I don't tell him the truth, which is that I bought the pills over the counter at a farmacia the last time I was in Cabo.

"Can you explain why you would take it first thing in the morning instead of bedtime?" Mr. Serious asks.

"I'm a vampire. I'm nocturnal," I reply.

I see pretty quickly that we're starting off on the wrong foot. I sometimes have a polarizing personality, and this guy is picking his pole. And it's not the pole that will be helpful to me, by the way. I hate that, because he is a looker.

My esquire shakes his head in exasperation or loathing, I cannot tell which, and walks to the front desk. I guess he's able to get everything "processed" because I am released. Turned loose back into society. I wave goodbye to my new friends in the holding tank, but neither responds in kind.

"Your car has been impounded as evidence," the lawyer tells me as he hands me my purse and a little freezer bag with all the contents from my jacket pocket that morning—gum, a used Kleenex, a loose Altoid that looks like a pill.

"You won't get it back until after the trial. The court date will be set next week."

Ouch. Nothing humorous comes to me to reply to that one. Trial? Court?

"Do you mind dropping me by my office?" I ask him. He seems torn about how to answer. There he is in a flawless, perfectly dry-cleaned dark suit and beautiful Prada wingtips. I'm sure my hair is jacked in the back and my skirt is slightly askew. I pat down my hair and straighten my clothes, giving him my best helpless girl look.

"I'm glad you called," he says. "I remember Tracey telling me that night we met how smart you are, what a great job you have at that PR agency. But now I don't know. This is serious, and I'm not sure you realize it. That woman is in the hospital."

"I know it's serious," I say. "Really. I hope she recovers quickly. I can't help my stupid mouth sometimes. Bad habit. I need your help, for real. I've never been in any kind of trouble, and this is all, I don't know…" I stammer.

He looks me in the eyes. I can tell he is weighing it all somewhere behind those steely blue pools. His prince charming good looks are the opposite of disarming. He makes me nervous.

"And who is Tracey?" I blurt out stupidly.

"Tracey is the girl who introduced us two months ago at that party? I was going out with her at the time. You went to college together?" I can feel his frustration with this entire morning.

Same, dude, same. He is slipping away for sure. "Tracey, right! Rough morning. I thought you might have meant someone here at the police station. Please—" I'm not above begging—"I need a ride to work, and I need you to help me out of this…this misunderstanding."

He caves. He opens the passenger door to his luxury sedan. Small version luxury, you know, like a starter series.

"Okay. I'll do it. But it's going to cost you, and we have some serious work to do to get you out of it." He motions for me to get in the car. It is the first decent thing that's happened to me all day, a ride to work with a good-looking guy.

I glance at the digital clock on his dash. "Shit. 12:30? I am so going to get nailed at work."

Mr. Hottie cuts his eyes toward me as he drives cautiously out of the lot. Both hands on the wheel, of course. His suit coat and shirt sleeve shift enough to expose his steel band Tag. I look down at my wrist and my third generation Apple Watch with a scratched face, hoping the time is different than his car clock. It is not.

"You haven't called anyone to explain what happened?" he asks.

"No. I decided against calling my Devil Wears Kmart boss from the jailhouse," I reply.

That one gets a little grin.

Look, I know I shouldn't be flirting with this guy, my lawyer or whatever. But his looks and his take-charge attitude are growing on me. I can't help myself. Maybe I'm just trying not to think about that woman and the funny way her leg was bent. I mean funny weird, not funny ha ha. Funny painful.

When we pull up to my office building, my attorney-turned-crush puts his blinker on and waits for me to get out of the car.

"So what happens from here?" I ask, thinking he might say we should grab dinner later or go away for the weekend.

"I need to check on your victim and get some paperwork together. I'll be in touch."

Ouch. My *victim*. That stung. I step out of his car, careful to shut the door without slamming it, and watch him drive away. I turn to face the music for being so damn late on a Monday.

BLAKE

I'm a bit shaken by the morning. So outside the norm for me. But exciting? Unhinged in a way that my life, and certainly my job, never is. *This one might actually be fun*, I think, a word I don't normally associate with my cases.

I grew up in Northern California, the only child of two small-town lawyers. My path was carved before I was born. Honestly, I never considered anything but the law. My parents have a good life. Rebellion never seemed necessary.

I did branch out and move to the big city though. I quickly found out that a fancier city only means fancier crooks. I like my work as a defense attorney, but I primarily defend white-collar criminals. It's more paperwork and less courtroom drama than you'd imagine, especially if you're a fan of *Law & Order* or any of its iterations. What I do is not that.

For months, I've been working day and night on a corporate merger that involves some pretty shady characters and some serious money laundering. No murder but also no morality. Guys like that hide their crimes in spreadsheets and documents. Nothing as brazen as running over a bicyclist.

Dark, I know, but I find myself loving the prospect of something different. It is a nice change of pace, even if it'll be a bit of a juggling act with my regular workload.

NIKKI

Devil Wears Kmart, or DK as I call her in my head, happens to be standing on the sidewalk when Mr. Wonderful drops me off, having what I am sure is her tenth cigarette of the day when I approach the front door. She makes a big deal of putting her arm to her face and looking at her fake Rolex as I wave to her. She's only ten years older than me but looks twenty thanks to the constant fire two inches from her face.

I hurry in and am greeted by a big whistle from Rachel, the receptionist, who I think is seriously twelve years old. "So, Nikki…walk of shame?" the child asks, her obnoxious phone headset perched on her head. Someone should tell her that less is more in the world of makeup. Or in the world in general.

"Definitely," I reply while rifling through the papers in my inbox at the edge of her desk.

"Looks like he has a nice car," she says, tapping her long manicured fake nails on her computer keyboard.

"Oh yes. Very nice. Attorney." I don't take her obvious bait and tell her more. I grab the contents of my box and head back to my office, kicking the door shut behind me.

"Shit. Shit Shit," I whisper to myself. I drop the mail and messages on my desk and fall into my chair. Through the window, I see DK take one last huge-ass pull off her Camel and flick it into the street. I know my second or third grilling of the day is about to begin.

Fuck it.

I check my social media. Even though I'm pretty sure each platform is run by Satan, I am drawn to them like an addict to heroin.

ALLISON

I have been "between jobs" for two years. That's what I call it. I guess it's closer to three years now. I was forty-two when my mother's Alzheimer's was diagnosed. Or at least that's when it got bad enough that my dad couldn't deal with it on his own anymore.

He asked me to dinner one night. Dinner without my mom. That was a new one. We met at Mijares in Pasadena. It's authentic Mexican. I've loved it since I was a girl, and later, I had my first margarita here. With my dad and my mom. It has always been our place as a family.

"Have you noticed anything new with Mom?" he began while we shared chips and salsa and waited for drinks.

"No," I answered, maybe a bit too quickly. I had noticed a few things.

The waiter brought our margaritas, and I paused, considering my answer.

"No Mrs. North tonight, eh? Father and daughter night?" the familiar server said.

My dad nodded in agreement.

"I take that back," I said. "She has repeated a few stories with me lately. But I do that too. I'm a bit forgetful."

Dad looked down at his glass and ran his finger across the salted rim.

"It's more than that," he says. "She gets lost. She misplaces her glasses, her phone. Last week she left the car running in the driveway all day. We saw a doctor, and it's bigger than forgetfulness. I'm afraid she can't really manage herself anymore."

I could see how hard it was for him to say this. He kept staring at his glass, unable to look at me. When he finally did, he smiled, although his eyes were moist.

"Ali, I have a proposition for you. How about you move back in with Mom and me? You can help her when I am not around. I'll pay you, and we can rent out your house so you can make money there too." He reached across the table and grabbed my arm in affection. Or maybe desperation.

I said yes immediately. I've never been all that career driven anyway, so it didn't seem like the biggest sacrifice to quit my job and help my mother. Plus, I could save some money. Spend more time with my parents. I didn't see a downside then.

At the time, I worked in a carpet store. I was what the old guys called an "office girl," although I'm not sure that moniker is allowed anymore. I started on the reception desk, directing customers to salesmen. And then I became a salesman, or saleswoman. I loved pulling the samples and discussing the patterns and designs. But carpet hasn't been in style for a long time. Fewer and fewer homeowners would come in looking, but more and more commercial building owners and church administrators did. Carpet became less about design and more about function, especially in a store like the one where I worked, which was more mom-and-pop than chic like all the designers use.

Long story short, no one really cared when I said I needed to quit my job to care for my mother. It felt like I saved them the trouble of firing me.

Caring for my mother, though, turned out to be much more taxing than selling floor coverings. My dad was always willing to help and would do whatever I asked, but he didn't exactly know what to do unless I told him.

Mom was fairly lucid for the first year after her diagnosis, so we spent part of each day playing cards or taking long walks. It really was the best "job" I'd ever had. I thought of it as a job because my dad paid me. He said it was only fair since I had given up my real job. I didn't protest. Plus, he was gone a lot, I mean *a lot,* during the day and even on weekends. I didn't really understand it, but I also didn't question it. It was like an extended slumber party with my mom. With pay.

I enjoyed this new job of hanging out with my mother. But eventually things changed. Mom became agitated easily. She developed a mean streak. The doctor told us it was a personality shift due to the Alzheimer's, that she couldn't help it. But no medical explanation changed the fact that the mom I knew was disappearing and being replaced with an angry old woman who looked a lot like my mother. An angry old woman who was now my job.

The first time something happened, she threw a lunch plate on the floor. She had asked me for tuna, and I made her a sandwich instead of placing it on the plate without bread.

"Not a sandwich, you dumb bitch. I said I want tuna fish salad!" she said, slamming the plate to the ground.

My mother would never lose her temper like that. She would never call me a bitch. And she would never throw dishes, especially her favorite blue ones with little yellow daisies.

And that wasn't an isolated incident.

I told my dad that we needed to move her out of the house. She needed more help than I could provide. Technically I guess I still could've managed it, but the heartbreak of dealing with this hateful woman who used to be my mother was more than I was willing to bear alone. Each day was Russian roulette, never knowing if we could quietly watch TV or if I would spend the day dodging her tantrums.

The facility we found offered round-the-clock care, and she also got her own private room. We tried to personalize it as much as we could. I brought some of her favorite art and books and scattered them on the walls and dresser. I may as well have hung blank frames and stacked empty journals. This new woman looked at them as though they meant nothing to her, these things that had meant so much to my mother.

Now I ride my bike to her assisted living facility every morning. I moved back to my house when my tenant's lease was up, but I'm still on my dad's payroll. I want to contribute somehow to earn that. And so I go visit her every day.

The best part of my day is the bicycle ride there and the return ride home. I bought a good quality bike with clips and gears and saddlebags. It's a luxury but also my respite. The rest of the day is spent in hours of heart-wrenching nonsensical talk with a woman I no longer know. She is softer there than she was at home. For some reason, she is less willing to break plates that don't belong to her. She isn't as mean, but she also isn't my mother.

Afterward comes the escape of the bike ride home. The sun on my face, wind blowing. Weaving in and out of traffic. I pretend this is my life and that I am young again. That part in the middle of the day, spent with my mother, is just a dream. A bad dream.

The Monday of the incident starts like most other mornings. I have been leaving my house later and later, perhaps avoiding the inevitable hours ahead, but also my mother sleeps later these days. What's left of the old her is shrinking, most likely only fully available when she's asleep. Sometimes Mom is still asleep when I arrive. Sometimes a nurse's aide is feeding her breakfast when I arrive.

I think about her schedule as I pedal slowly when I suddenly feel the car bumper on my back tire. I actually think it's a dog at first. It's just sort of a graze, not a big impact. But when I turn my head and see a car right behind me, I lose it.

All the rage I've been feeling about my mother roars out, and I uncharacteristically throw a middle finger at the driver. In doing so, I lose control of the handlebars and fall My cycling shoes are still clipped in, or at least one is, and that one twists in a direction it shouldn't twist, causing a popping sound that makes me want to pass out.

Did I pass out? I'm not sure, but when I open my eyes, the car is gone and my leg is turned in an impossible direction. I hear a siren. I keep my eyes closed. *Someone should call my mother and tell her I'm not coming.* But when the medic asks if they can call someone for me, I say no. Because really, my mother no longer exists.

NIKKI

I am twenty-eight. Six years into what I once thought was my dream job. I'm a publicist for an entertainment PR firm. I started at reception a year or so after college. My degree is in communications, so public relations seemed like a magical fit. I worked my way up to junior publicist, and now I have my own client list.

That first year after college, before I got the "real" job, I waited tables and tended bar and generally loved my life. Now? Well, be careful what you ask for—unless you want soul suicide one day at a time. I'm not sure why we all rush into adulthood for this.

Have you ever been in the Beverly Center Macy's? A guy in there sells shoes and he seems so damn happy. Not even in an annoying way. It's like he enjoys his job and his life. Weirdo. The guy seems oblivious to the kind of shit that drives the rest of us crazy. I often wish I could be like that. Oblivious.

I grew up in LA. I am a unicorn. Most people move to Los Angeles to become a star—an actor or some kind of entertainer. Let's call a spade a spade—people move here to become famous. But my mother moved here way back when from the middle-of-nowhere Kansas to follow a man, dragging my perfect brother and me with her. That man turned out to be bad news, as did at least three stepfathers after that. But we're all still here, my mother, my brother, and me. My mother works in the same insurance office that hired her however many years ago, and my perfect brother and his perfect wife live in the suburbs, where he works as a perfect CPA. Perfectly boring.

My mother has now given up on men altogether and seems to be having some sort of relationship with her friend Alice, although none of us actually talk about it. Alice is always around, and I'm starting to think she may even live at my mother's house.

One time I stopped by my mother's house so she could tell me all the ways I disappoint her. Okay, that's not why I went, but that's what I got. Anyway, Alice pulled me aside and said, "I love your mother."

"Me too," I replied.

"No. I *really* love your mother," Alice said.

Message received.

My brother, Perfect Glenn, was already perfect when we were kids. Or at least my mother thought so. He could do no wrong in her eyes. But when the two of us were alone? Not so much. He liked to wrestle with me, which I'm sure all kids do. But he was four years older than me. And had a penis. At some point, that was not cool, you know? Like when he was sixteen and I was twelve, and he pressed his boner into my back while he held me down. Gross! I did not even know what it was exactly, but I somehow knew it was wrong.

He would also race me home from school so he could lock me out of the house. So what? We lived in Southern Cali. It wasn't like I had to sit in the snow. Idiot. He would let me inside right before Mom got home. "I'll knock your teeth out if you tell."

I never told. I had grown fond of my teeth.

This is the difference between men and women. A steakhouse in Texas has a nightly contest involving a seventy-two-ounce steak and a clock. You have to eat the entire thing in an hour, along with the accompanying sides—all for the "prize" of getting the meal for free. That's the prize? Doing something that makes you want to vomit? Try to guess how many women enter this contest.

Where is my father in all of this? Dead. I could sugarcoat it and say "in heaven" or "he passed." I don't get the whole "passing" thing. Like we're all on some highway and these people have passed us? They're dead. In the ground or maybe burned to a crisp like my father. But no one says that: "Oh, he stopped breathing so we had his body burned."

My father died when I was young. So young that I barely have any memories of him. I remember taking a sip of his beer. I remember sitting on his lap in the front seat and steering the wheel. But mainly, I remember the aftermath. My brother saying that *he* was the man of the house since Dad was gone. *Gone*. Like there was a possibility he would come back. Like I said, my father is dead.

I didn't know how he died when it first happened. That's how young I was. No one tells a four-year-old about suicide. I guess they tell eight-year-olds though, because Glenn knew and ended up telling me about it two years later. We were at a birthday party. The birthday girl, Penny O'Brien, was my friend, so the party was a bunch of six-year-old girls. Penny had an older brother, Ryan, who was in Glenn's class at school. Their mother had invited Glenn to come play with Ryan while the party was going on. After the cake and games and gifts, one by one, moms and dads came and picked up each of their little girls. Eventually only Glenn and I were left.

I found him sniveling on the front porch.

"What's wrong, Glenn?" I asked him. It scared me to see him cry.

"Mom's not here!" he shouted at me. "She's not here! She should be here by now!"

I thought I might cry too. Were we going to be left to live at the O'Briens'? I didn't have my clothes or toys.

"She'll be here," I told him in my most grown-up six-year-old voice, trying hard to believe that what I said was true.

"What if she shot herself like Daddy did?" he said between tears.

I looked at him and knew he was telling the truth. Daddy being dead was just a fact of life at that point, and I never questioned it. Now I had a million questions and no one to ask. Not Glenn, who was too upset about it. And not my mother, who very well could be dead too.

Mom pulled up in the driveway moments later, driving stepfather number one's car. The reason we had come to Los Angeles. She appeared to still be alive.

***

Growing up in LA is…well, it's all I knew. We went to public school, so it wasn't like we were surrounded by child actors, not successful ones anyway. A lot of kids had struggling artists for parents, also known as waiters. No one had much money, and we all ran around doing the same kind of bullshit all you other people growing up in Nowhere, USA, did. But of course, we assumed we were cooler—because we were from California.

One time, Brian Keller, who in my opinion was the hottest boy in seventh grade, told me I was cuter than the other acne-stricken, small-boobed preadolescents in our class. Not his exact words, but you get the idea. He stuck his tongue down my throat. It was awkward because I was about a full foot taller than he was, and I had to lean way down for him to get in there. We were at Belinda Moriarty's house. She was in the kitchen making microwave popcorn. I hoped she might burn it so he'd have time to do it again. Later she told me he did the same thing to her when I went to the bathroom. Some kind of player, that Brian.

I was too clumsy to be good at sports and too hipster to be a cheerleader. I honed my cynicism and read dark novels and pined for older boys. My brother's irreverent erections and Brian's groping aside, I held onto my virginity all through high school, at least what we called virginity. You know, everything but. No BUTT! Everything but. I assumed my girlfriends did too. Turns out some did and some didn't. Hormones and rubbing. It's all the same outcome. We are illusionists when it comes to telling our stories, changing the narrative and the timelines to fit the audience. Especially when it comes to sex.

College was cool. I didn't go far. UCLA—go Bruins! It took me four and a half years, but I got the piece of paper.

Since college, I've had a recurring dream that I killed someone and the body I hid is discovered. A construction site maybe. Or under my house. No one ever suspects me, but I am silently panicked. And when I wake up, part of me believes it's true, that there really is a body hidden underneath my house.

There is of course. Not a physical body but deceptions and betrayals. Regrets. Things I have buried with the hopes that no one will come digging. Mainly stupid stuff. Embarrassing stuff. Stuff that would mean nothing to anyone but me. Most of this stuff happened in college.

Another thing that still haunts me from my UCLA days is Sunday nights—that time when people would return from their weekends at home. Homes that seemed purer and more blessed than my own for some reason. Norman Rockwell compared to my Salinger-skewed. That's another thing no one tells you about—the weird melancholy that first appears in college and stays with you after that (or it has so far anyway).

The Sunday scaries.

Minus Sundays, those were some great years. It's when I met Tracey after all, who had the decency to remember me and to introduce me to the attorney.

And that attorney may end up being my knight in shining armor regarding this whole hit-and-run thing. Can you believe they're calling it that?

Tracey was in my sorority. I know I might not come across as the sorority type, and I didn't stay in all four and a half years. But I did pledge. I wanted to prove to myself that I could get in. And I did. Turns out, I didn't bond with my sisters for the long haul. I was better at frat parties than sorority meetings.

Beth, our chapter president, pulled me aside one night after a meeting.

"Look Nikki, all those cute comments you make in there? No one thinks you're funny," she said. "This is about our sisterhood! You're acting like a clown." The seriousness on her face made it seem as if we had been discussing global politics rather than homecoming floats.

As one of my boyfriends once said, "If you can't laugh at yourself, you probably won't be friends with Nikki." Those sorority girls took themselves pretty damn seriously.

***

DK barges into my office without knocking so I'm forced to fumble around to close TikTok and pretend I'm working. She plops into a chair across from my desk, her junior dress hiking up over her missy thighs.

"New hours, Nikki?" she asks.

"I am so sorry. I got sidetracked this morning."

"Oh, I *saw* Mr. Sidetrack drop you off out front. Hope he's worth it." DK grins like a sick, sadistic Cheshire cat.

Since she wants to think I whored it up and spent my morning in a more pleasurable way than running over geriatric bicyclists, I go with it.

"Soooo worth it. I hope you understand. And he's an attorney. A real keeper." I wink at her.

Here's the thing about DK. She's a total bitch when she thinks you're trying to pull one over on her. But if you act like she's your girlfriend and part of some sort of slutty scheme, she is all in.

"Well, good for you! You need to get laid more often." She pulls at the cheap fabric of her dress until finally giving in and standing to get it back covering what it's meant to cover.

"Just don't make a habit of it. Coming in late, I mean." She exits in a cloud of vanilla musk and cigarette smoke, leaving me to get back to the talking dog video I was watching on my phone before DK blessed me with her presence.

Maybe I should friend my new attorney on Facebook, old school. What's his last name again? I pull out his card to make sure I get the spelling right. Hoynacki. Yuck. Guess I'll keep my maiden name after we're married. I'll never be able to sign that albatross.

Blake Hoynacki. Half hot name, half mouthful. His Facebook picture must be his office headshot, stoic but still handsome. I need to teach him how to use the AI apps that make your photos better than reality. Judging from the way he looked this morning, his reality is pretty damn good.

I click "Add friend" and move on to see what's on Page Six.

One good thing about my job—okay, maybe there's more than one good thing—is that I have to check out all the gossip sites and rags daily. I'm looking for mentions of my clients obviously, but I'm also keeping up with the Kardashians of the world. Don't ask me how the stock market is doing, but I can tell you what KK wore last night.

I have three clients I'm responsible for publicizing. One is a teen with a momager. Mom wants all the fame and the invites and gifts that come with it. The kid hates all of it, but he does whatever Mama wants to make her happy. She holds on to him so tight, so convinced that he isn't ready or able to be an adult without her that she makes it so.

Once, when Mama was on the phone and we had two seconds alone, the boy confided that he wants to be a normal kid. Good for him. Maybe he'll find the balls, once his drop, to kick Momager's ass to the curb. Meanwhile, it's up to me to get him to all the G-rated openings and wholesome events I can find so he doesn't stray too far from the squeaky-clean kid he plays on a sitcom.

I also have a soap star, or *former* soap star, on my client roster. Since that format is hanging on by a thread, this girl reads for every part her agent can find. I'm supposed to keep her relevant by getting her into the hot clubs and VIP parties. She's good but is starting to get a little desperate. I sense a porn movie in her future.

The star of my client list, and the only reason DK keeps me here, is Axel Miller. He is the real deal. He gets his name above the title now. He is in "films." He also is the son of stepfather number two, which is the reason I was able to sign him in the first place. I don't consider him a brother, mainly because my real brother is such a dick, but he was a great hang for those couple years when we were related by marriage. And he has always stayed in my life.

We made out once. Drunk groping when we were both teenagers, not long after our parents divorced. We ended up getting the giggles and that was that, zero chemistry. But he has stayed a friend and saved my life by signing with me when I was trying to get ahead in this job. He also gave me the down payment for my condo, a bonus when he earned his first backend on a movie. He said I earned it. We both knew that wasn't true, but I took it.

After searching online for mentions of my clients, or no mentions of my clients as it turns out, I turn back to finding a way out of today's nightmare.

I Google "hit-and-run" and "bad leg breaks." I don't know what the hell I'm looking for. Truthfully, I could use the other half of that Xanax about right now. It's a shame I left it at home. But also it's a good thing Tiny didn't find it during her strip search. *Basically* a strip search. I feel violated anyway.

Hit and Run is the name of a Dax Shepard movie, so I get sucked into reading about that and forget all about what I'm doing. When I check out "bad leg breaks," I cringe. *Yikes*. There are definitely some pictures you don't want to see there.

Next I Google my name in case it has somehow gotten out what happened this morning, instead of the walk of shame DK assumed. Same shit pops up about my clients and me. Nothing new or more damaging than the usual. No new public arrest photos. Thank God.

My email inbox dings, and I see that the sender is Blake Hoynacki. For about the five hundredth time in the past six years, I wonder if DK monitors our office email.

Blake doesn't start his email with some cute "Hey" or "Hello" like a normal person. "Your victim, Allison North, has been released from the hospital," he abruptly states.

Well, that is fantastic news! How bad could it possibly be if that crazy bitch was already released? Looks like I can forget about vehicular manslaughter as a charge. Why the hell isn't my attorney offering a congratulations or something like that?

He signs, "Regards, BH."

Regards? What's that supposed to mean? Am I even in trouble? Can we go ahead and get this whole thing tossed? I mean, Ms. Cyclist is fine! Probably rode her bike home!

Just when I'm about to convince myself that this worst-ever Monday morning could easily be erased, he of few words sends another email.

"We need to set a time tomorrow for you to come to my office and discuss the charges against you. Regards, BH."

Regards again! Charges? Fuck.

Why is it *charges* multiple? Shouldn't it be one charge if anything? Allison is back out there racing the streets on her two-wheeled death trap. Why do I have charges?

That's how I can turn it. That's how I can look at it. Maybe I'm the one who should have been a lawyer. I am a spin master after all. A publicist is basically a lawyer without the extra three years of graduate school if you ask me. Also without the attorney paycheck.

I turn to the appointment book on my desk to see what tomorrow's schedule looks like. I have a photoshoot with Axel for the cover of a men's magazine. I need to be there at 9 a.m., and who knows how long it will go. He'll do the shoot and then sit for an interview after that. It's a long profile, so it could take a while.

"Tomorrow is booked solid for me. Can it wait a day?" I reply to my new boyfriend. I sign my email, "X, Nikki." That's sort of a habit, my standard sign-off. I dropped the *O* when I got the adult job but hung on to the *X*. Which one stands for a kiss, the X or the O? Either way, I like giving people a little something with my name. Especially Mr. Stick-Up-His-Ass.

Ten minutes go by with nothing, and then the twelve-year-old from the front desk rings in to tell me a Mr. Hoynacki is on the phone.

"This is Nikki," I say as I pick up.

"Blake Hoynacki. I am not sure you get this. You must meet with me right away. You're lucky you are not in jail right now!"

I can tell Mr. Hoynacki is slightly perturbed.

"Oh hi, Blake. I'm a very lucky girl. I was just saying that myself. Sounds like you're dying to see me?" I smile into the phone.

Based on the dead silence on the other end, I don't believe my new lawyer is doing the same.

I try again. "I absolutely understand. But I have an all-day commitment for work tomorrow."

He cuts me off. "What time do you start?"

"9 a.m. in Burbank," I reply.

"Fine. Be at my office at 7 a.m.," he responds. "And have you thought about alternative transportation?"

Crap. That's right. My car is impounded. I haven't considered how I'm going to get around. I guess asking this guy to be my driver isn't going to work, but I do like that he asked. Taking care of me in that boyfriend way already.

"Well, if you're offering to give me a ride, that's okay. Don't worry about it. I have it covered. I'll see you at 7." I can be quick and efficient too. And I can lie.

We hang up. I Google car rentals in Los Angeles. I can already feel the money being sucked out of my wallet over this whole ridiculous ordeal. And it looks like I might have to Uber all the way to the airport to pick up the cheapest car.

When I was ten, I was the lead in the school play. Not that I ever wanted to be an actress, but this was a big damn deal. It was a Mother's Day play, and I was the mother. Looking back, I think it might have been because I already had breasts and the other girls did not, but at the time, I was convinced that my thespian ability, not my training bra, was carrying the whole show.

Anyway, Alice's girlfriend, only known as my mom at that time, decided at the last minute not to go. She had a date with some new guy that night, and besides, wasn't I old enough to do this on my own?

I was. I am. I suck it up and continue my search for car rental agencies. No car is available until tomorrow. I'm batting a thousand in terms of best-ever Mondays.

***

On Tuesday, my iPhone alarm works. It blares at 4:30 a.m., not that I need it. I was awake all night. Watching reruns of *Rosanne*. Forcing myself to not take my usual ibuprofen PM for fear that I would screw up this day too.

After a questionable trip in an Uber that smelled like last night's booze fest, I fold myself into my rental by 5:45 a.m. A green Kia. How far I've fallen, and already I regret the stick shift. It seemed like a good way to save a little cash yesterday when I reserved the car. How am I going to drink my coffee and also change gears? Dammit.

I pull into Blake's office garage right at 6:59 a.m. Traffic was a little worse than expected, and I feel every pothole in this car. I think there's more coffee on the floorboard than in me.

His is one of those super secure buildings where I have to get my photo taken at the front desk and wait for a badge and clearance to go up to the twelfth floor. When the elevator doors finally open at the law firm, my phone says 7:06. I'm sure my new love won't be thrilled about that.

Blake stands at the reception desk, hands in his steel-gray suit pockets, looking very stern. He also looks pretty hot again. Attractive in a not-in-the-entertainment-business kind of way. His hair is slightly damp, and his face is freshly shaved. Crisp all around. I suddenly feel childish in my photoshoot day athleisure attire—a bright blue tracksuit complete with racing stripes down the legs and sleeves. Sneakers. And a baseball hat to top it all off.

"The receptionist doesn't come in until eight, so I thought I should meet you up front," he says. "I've been waiting."

"Great to see you too!" I jump in before he can go on. "I didn't expect the inquisition and photo op downstairs. Basically I'm two for two starting my day with a mug shot this week. All good with you?"

"Come on back." He turns away from the desk.

Damn, this guy is rigid. That mug shot joke was a total failure.

Blake's office is extremely modern. White on white on white. No photos or color at all except his black leather desk chair, if you consider that color. I sit in a chrome and white plastic version across from him, looking like a Smurf in my exercise clothes.

"Do you think I could get a cup of coffee before we get into this?" I ask.

"Sorry, I'm not sure any has been made yet. I'll check." He walks around the desk and heads to the office door.

"You don't drink it?" I ask.

"Not my thing," he says over his shoulder as he disappears.

He returns with a white mug and hands it to me—before I have enough time to search his desk.

"So what *is* your thing?" I ask over the steaming black liquid.

He returns to his chair behind the desk. "Excuse me?"

"You said coffee isn't your thing. What is your thing?" I try to make this all light and fun.

He ignores my effort.

"It's good you didn't take the breathalyzer test. What made you do that?" Mr. Business redirects the conversation.

"Reflex, I think. I've always heard not to take it so you don't create evidence against you if you're stopped for a DUI. Obviously, I wasn't drinking and this wasn't a DUI stop, but still. It didn't seem like I should give them anything." I shrug. "Although maybe I should have shared my Xanax with Tiny."

Blake doesn't laugh at my joke.

"Well, like I said, that's good. And there is no mention of intoxication on the police report. Apparently you convinced Officer Martinez," he says as he scans a paper on his desk.

"Who?"

"I think she's the woman you're calling 'Tiny.'" He almost grins.

Ha! He does get me! Although I'm not sure he appreciates my Tiny Xanax joke.

"Look, you are extremely lucky," he continues. "Let's forget about the Xanax, and I suggest you never mention it to anyone else."

"Attorney-client privilege?"

"Something like that. Also, there was a witness, a pedestrian on the sidewalk. That may or may not be a problem. He says the bicycle swerved in front of you. But he also says it sounded like you gunned the car after you hit her. Did you?"

Fuck. I don't say that out loud, and I don't know how I keep it in, but I'm trying to be as serious as he is.

"That is my stupid car! I swear, the transmission hangs and jumps all on its own sometimes. I in no way meant to gun it after tapping her. Barely tapping her," I add.

"The big issue is leaving the scene of the accident. Why did you keep going?" he asks.

"Have you ever been on that street? It's totally residential with cars parked on both sides. There was nowhere to pull over. I had to circle the block to get back to her," I whine to him.

"Why not stop there, right where you hit her?" Blake interjects.

"Too slow because of the Xanax?"

I regret saying it as soon as it leaves my mouth. I told you my brain can't keep up sometimes, especially at this ungodly hour.

He doesn't respond but looks at me intently. Stares me down from across that white behemoth of a desk. It's like the look a teacher would give you for speaking out of turn in class. Not that I have ever experienced that, of course.

"I don't know. I don't think to stop in the middle of the street. Like ever. You know?" I balk.

He looks back down at whatever that paper is on his desk, inside an open folder.

"What is that anyway? My file or something? Can I see it?" I question him.

He closes the black glossy folder.

"I guess bad guys go in black folders. I assume the good guys' folders are all white?" I inquire.

Not even a smile. He slides it over to me.

I open it up and the first thing I see is my photo from yesterday's booking. It is comical really. There is a flyaway hair thing happening, a result of being scrunched down in the back seat trying to find some level of comfort with my hands cuffed behind my back. I'm not smiling, and in fact, look like I'm smelling something atrocious, nostrils flaring. Probably that toilet in the holding cell.

"Well, I certainly look the part of a deranged driver," I say. "What's that I'm smelling?"

Mr. Serious actually smiles.

"Okay," I close the file. "Just tell me what to do from here please." I give him my most sincere look.

"Would you like to know about the victim?"

There was that word again. *Victim.*

"Yes. Allison. Home already and on the mend, I guess?" I offer hesitantly.

"Home, yes. Not exactly on the mend. In a cast from her pelvis to her heel for at least six weeks. Then, therapy. Then—"

"Shit!" I cut him off. "That's more than I expected. I guess I'm going to pay for that?"

"You are absolutely going to pay for it financially. You and your insurance company, if they'll even accept it as an accident claim. Also, if they don't drop you altogether for the hit-and-run aspect of this. That is usually a policy voider. Your bigger issue is legal. You could be looking at jail or a lost license or both. Or worse."

Wasn't he supposed to be on my side? I sit in silence for once in my life. I feel redness creeping up my neck and suddenly it feels very hot in here. A lump forms in my throat. I struggle to find a humorous comeback.

I stand abruptly and tell Blake "Okay, I've got to get to this photoshoot. You tell me what I have to do and I'll do it."

He looks up at me from behind that sea of white. I am not sure if it's compassion or confusion I see in his deep-set blue eyes.

"Well, there is one thing. She, Allison North, could decide not to press charges. She could tell the police it was a no-fault accident and that she was in shock at the scene. Somehow relieve you of any responsibility. Only criminal responsibility. You'd still be liable for all her medical expenses no matter what."

See? This is the kind of thing I've been looking for. Some hope. Some way to put this whole thing behind me. I swallow the growing blockage in my throat.

"Done and done!" I am already halfway to his office door. "'ll do whatever she needs. You let me know!" The last thing I want to do is have this guy see my cry.

"Thanks for the coffee! Call me!" I blurt out as I race down the hall.

And I'm gone. Back to my world of color.

I had to get out of there. I don't like crying. Not in front of other people. Of course, I've had my moments—full on fetal position wailers—but never in front of anyone if I can help it.

The night my mother first introduced me to Stepfather number 1, I was having two girlfriends over for a sleepover. They were my favorite two friends—okay, my only two new friends—from the school year. Fourth grade, I think?

I remember when Mom told me he'd be there for dinner. They weren't married then. It was just some boyfriend of my mother's coming to dinner with my friends there. I was mortified! These girls had real dads, alive ones who were still married to their real mothers. That's pretty much the night I decided to be a smart-ass. I didn't call it that at the time, but I thought,"*I'll make the jokes here.* Beat everyone to the punch. Act like this is perfectly normal, fun even, to have strange men over for dinner. What a hoot!

I am proud of this skill. At times, it serves me well. More so than tears.

***

As always, Axel is a dream. His shots are gorgeous, but even better than his unblemished beauty, Axel keeps us all laughing. You go on enough of these things, and you know the whole day can be ruined if the subject is a diva. All of us behind the scenes—publicists, managers, crew, glam squads—feed off the center of our world for the day. Celebrities in bad moods equal bad photo shoots, bad interviews, bad scenes. You name it. A bad day in general. That is never a concern with Axel. Not yet anyway. As fast as his star is rising, I suppose there's plenty of time. He could always turn into a prick.

Of course, DK shows up unannounced. "Dropping by to say hi to our favorite client," she says as she squeezes the life out of poor Axel.

He is irresistible. At some point, it dawns on me, what if his charm can once again come to my rescue?

I scroll through my phone between photo setups and Google my victim. Nothing crazy jumps out.

I find her Facebook.

You wouldn't believe the post she has written about how some bitch ran her over! Clicking through to her info page, I find it. There, exactly what I need to see. On her list of favorite celebrities, Axel Miller!

I go through the rest of the day with a smirk on my face, like I have solved the world's biggest dilemma. I am a problem-solving genius. I should apply my skills to world peace.

At some point, I send Mr. Serious a text. Maybe he'll be less formal in text. "All figured out. I can make this whole thing go away." I add a smiley face emoji. Too much?

He sends back, after *many* minutes, "?"

Man of Few Words is even briefer in text.

"Call u ltr." That's about as short as I can get. No smiley face.

BLAKE

I'm in a client meeting when I see Nikki's text. I should not be looking at my phone, but I can't help myself. I respond to her. I have not stopped thinking about her all day, ever since she left my office in practically a full-on run. I find her to be so cool and funny, but this morning there was a glimpse of something else. Vulnerability? I catch myself smiling. Definitely not my normal start to a morning, much like yesterday. I see her "call u ltr" and return my attention to the client in front of me.

Mostly.

I had a date last night. Dinner with a new woman I met at the gym, Ashley Something. We never say much beyond hello at the gym, but I enjoy seeing her there. We have the same schedule it seems, at least as far as the gym goes.

At dinner, she asks a million questions about my work, tells me all about hers. She sells pharmaceuticals. She orders a salad she never eats. I don't laugh once.

NIKKI

When the shoot is done and the interview finished, I follow Axel to his dressing room. He pulls off his denim button-up, exposing the chest and abs America has fallen in love with. As he leans over the sink to wash off his makeup, I grab him from behind and wrap my arms around his waist. Not professional, I know, but as I said, this guy was once upon a time a stepbrother to me.

"Great day." My cheek is pressed against his shoulder blade. "Can I buy you a drink and burden you with my problems?"

I realize that most women would give anything to be in this position. DK would for sure lose her shit.

The warmth of his smooth skin against my face is comforting in a way that nothing else has been this week. He shakes me off, in that brotherly way. I throw myself on the couch and prop my feet up on the small table positioned in front it, smudging the pile of headshots he has stacked there. A Nike imprint now resides on his chin in the top photo.

"I'm in," he grins. "But what now?"

"Now? What is that supposed to mean?" I genuinely ask.

"You need a loan? A boyfriend hurt your feelings? You'll get fired if I don't pose for the cover of *Playgirl* online? Any of these ring a bell?" he asks while pulling on a deep gray V-neck T-shirt over his head. I know he's teasing me, but he's not wrong.

This one, however, has slightly bigger consequences than those very real problems. Real, I know, because they happened to me. This one could mean losing my license or going to jail or whatever else Blake insinuated. Like losing my insurance. No need to tell Axel all of that. Yet.

"Just a little traffic accident. Nothing tragic or major," I tell him.

We walk out to the parking lot where my car sits next to his pristine Porsche. He doubles over in laughter as he walks around my little Kia, examining it. It looks like something that could have fallen out of his tailpipe, except for the screaming neon lime color.

"Wow, nice wheels," he laughs. "I guess I should feel like an asshole when this is the best my publicist can drive."

"It's a rental," I reply.

"Obviously. Is that the only color they had available?" He can't stop laughing. "Look, ride with me. I don't want to be seen with you getting out of that thing." He acts like he's kidding, but I think there's a seed of truth in there.

I climb into his passenger seat, the sheen of my tracksuit sliding easily across the leather, and we go tearing onto the freeway, about ten times faster than I was moving when I hit my so-called victim.

He pulls up to this hole-in-the-wall bar.

The reason people like Axel make so much money isn't because they're remarkably talented. It's because of all the fame shit they have to put up with. I wouldn't wish fame on my worst enemy. There is no turning it off. Once you have agreed to pursue it, your life is an open book. Forever. There is no putting the genie back in the bottle. You wouldn't believe the crap we'd go through if we went somewhere halfway decent, where people recognized Axel. In a bar like this, most of the clientele are hiding out from something or someone. No one even looks our way.

Old country music plays through scratchy speakers. Something about family tradition. Smoke from a bygone era clings to the paneled interior walls. Peeling leatherette barstools line a dark bar. It's crusty but endearing. A perfect setup for some clandestine meeting. I doubt I'm the first woman he has brought here.

We both slump into a booth near the back, and I order a Jack neat.

"Whiskey? Must be some story," Axel says. He orders a vodka soda.

"I'm not sure this place has a great wine list," I retort.

We make small talk about the photoshoot until the waitress is back with our drinks. If she recognizes him, she doesn't show it.

"I had a minor car accident yesterday…" I begin.

"So that's why you have the rental," he says. "How minor?"

"I may have hit a woman on a bicycle with my car." I shoot back a hefty gulp of Jack.

"What?" Axel hasn't touched his drink yet. "You consider that minor?"

"Okay, it's not *minor*, I guess. But I wouldn't call it major. She's going to be okay—"

Axel waits me out.

"Eventually," I add. "She did break her leg. And there's some confusion about whether I left the scene—even though I didn't go far!" I glance at him. "I could lose my driver's license…"

Axel takes his first sip of vodka.

"But...she's a *big* Axel Miller fan," I say, gauging the look on his face.

Axel leans back as if settling in to hear my story.

In this version, I take out the references to Mr. Cutie Lawyer, except to say that I have an attorney and he is very good.

"Let's cut to the chase. How exactly do you think I can help?" Axel asks.

"I checked out this woman's Facebook today, and of course she has a big thumbs up on Axel Miller." I smile at him, downing the last of my drink.

"Aha!" He raises his glass to me and finishes the last of his girly drink..

"So do I need to sleep with her? Sign her cast?" he asks. He makes the check sign gesture to summon the waitress back. Even though I said I'd buy the drinks, he never allows that. I should have ordered dinner too.

"Somewhere in the middle of those two things should work. However, if quasi-crippled middle-aged chicks turn out to be your thing, have I got the girl for you," I reply.

Relief and the warmth of the whiskey flood through me. I can see the light at the end of this accident ordeal. We roll down the windows of the Porsche on the way back to my car and turn up the music. I am sixteen again.

I wait until I'm home to call Mr. Hoynacki. I consider what to tell him on my drive home in the Kia, going way slower than I would normally drive. I cling to ten and two to be doubly sure I don't rack up any more "victims." I kick off my shoes once I'm in the door and dial his number.

"Hoynacki."

"Hey, Blake. It's your favorite client. Have you missed me?"

Nothing on the other end.

I continue. "I happened to notice on Facebook today that Allison, my *victim*, is a big fan of one of my clients," I say as I walk through my condo, closing blinds, turning on lights.

"Really? Who?"

Ah. I have his attention.

"Axel Miller," I reply. I look in the bathroom mirror and give myself a self-satisfied smile now that I have delivered the winning card to my lawyer. I pull off my baseball cap and shake out my long brown hair, flattened by the day.

"*The* Axel Miller? The movie star? He's your client?" He seems to not really believe this, like it might be another joke in my long line of zingers.

"He is. He's an old family friend and my client. I talked to him about helping me out. He's willing to do whatever we need."

The other end of the call is silent.

The problem with being such a smart-ass is that sometimes people waver on whether you're yet again joking or actually telling the truth. Once, I fell at a party and tore my ACL. Everyone thought I was kidding around again, playing drunk, funny Nikki—until I couldn't stand up.

"He's honestly willing to meet her or do whatever he has to," I go on in my most earnest voice, pacing in my tiny galley kitchen.

"Okay," he says. "Maybe that's helpful. I don't really see how though. But maybe," Blake trails off. He obviously hasn't seen the power of fame like I have.

"Trust me. If this woman is into Axel enough to post about it on her socials, I think he can probably charm the pants off her in person," I say. "Not that it'll come to that, but I am sure he can charm her into dropping the charges or whatever you said this morning." I open the refrigerator, finding only cottage cheese, Diet Coke, beer, and pickles. Not exactly the meal I was hoping for.

Again, nothing from Hottie at the other end of the line.

"Look, I've seen girls take their shirts off to get his attention. If we work out a legit meeting, coffee or something for her with Axel, this is a done deal." I move on to the kitchen cabinets without much success. I finally settle on a Cliff bar.

Still nothing from Blake.

"It's at least worth a try. If it doesn't work, I'll either turn myself in or go on the run," I continue. To me, this seems like the easiest solution in the world, but it appears I'm speaking Greek to my new esquire.

"Okay," he finally answers. "I need to reach out to her and see if she's open to it."

Finally. Now we're getting somewhere.

"Here is what we need to do," I say. "You set up a meeting with her. Only you and her. Based on my experience, she'll freak out if you tell her Axel is going to be there. So set up something for the two of you, and Axel and I will show up. He'll pose for pics, tell her how great I am, and this whole thing will be over."

The tables have turned. Now *I'm* the one taking charge. All business, no jokes.

"Okay. It's your case," he says. "If this is how you want to move forward, I'll arrange for a meeting. I'll draw up all the paperwork we'll need to get this cleaned up as much as possible. I'll get a statement from that witness too. That will help. The meeting may have to be at her house though. I don't see how I can ask her to travel in her condition."

Condition. That's almost as bad as *victim.* It makes it sound like she's not only hurt but also pregnant. That can't be true. She's a hundred years old and definitely not boning anyone. Her being with child would require a star to appear in the east.

After a few more rounds of Blake's doubts and my insistence, we leave it that BH is going to call Allison and ask if he can come by her house to see her. I hope beyond hope that she doesn't have a lawyer of her own yet. Surely she hasn't had time to find one. I only found one quickly because I needed a "get out of jail free" card. A lawyer might not be as easily swayed by Axel as I'm sure Allison will be.

I hang up the phone and plop down on my couch with a Diet Coke and the Cliff bar. I decide my solution to this issue is worthy of a bigger celebration and order a pizza instead.

On Tuesday night, I sleep like a baby.

BLAKE

I make the call, schedule the appointment. I don't really believe it'll work, but Nikki is the client. It's my job to deliver. She was adamant that this was her choice. Allison North agrees to meet. There's a chance, I suppose.

I stare at the ceiling Tuesday night. My white noise machine hums, my blackout shades are fully extended, but I can't sleep. I can't believe how often I think about this girl who mostly drives me crazy. Also, I get to see her again this week.

Ashley, the girl from Monday night, left me a voice mail today. I still haven't listened to it.

ALLISON

I'm counting out Loratabs when the phone rings. If I'm supposed to take one every four hours, I rationalize that one every six hours, with a glass of wine in between, will work the same. I can pull myself off the couch and hobble to the bathroom on crutches pretty easily. That's all I need to do for now. I definitely can't drive. Who knows when I'll be able to do that. Getting back on the bike seems like a long-term improbability. Since the heaviest machinery I currently operate is the TV remote, I can manage wine and painkillers.

My pride is probably more wounded than my leg. But I'm hurt bad enough that I still plan on taking Daddy's money even though I'm zero help to him or my mom for now.

I don't recognize the number, but I answer anyway. I'll take whatever human connection I can get at this point.

"Ms. North? This is Blake Hoynacki. I represent Nikki Carpenter. I'm sorry for calling so late," he says. I know from the newscast on the TV screen that it's sometime after 6:00.

"Nikki who?" I respond, thinking my mind must be fuzzier than I thought with these meds.

"Nikki Carpenter. The woman who was involved in your traffic accident."

"By *accident*, do you mean the woman who ran over me and left me for dead?" I hear my words slur a bit as I snap back at him. But this guy doesn't know me. Maybe this is how I talk all the time. Juno, my orange tabby, jumps onto my lap and knocks the pain pills out of my hand. Some bounce off my cast and roll to the floor.

My renter begged me to take the cat before he left. He said his new landlord didn't allow pets and the cat was so at home in my house. He swore she was no trouble. I have never had a pet but thought what the hell. That guy didn't seem like the best pet owner if he was so willing to give up the cat. I was sure she'd be better off with me than him. Living back at my parents' place, I had become accustomed to having someone around. Something with a pulse.

Juno has been a good companion. More cognizant than my mother and more present than my father.

"I need to go," I mutter into the phone, struggling to get the pills before the cat does.

"Can I come by your house and see you Thursday afternoon?" this guy asks.

I say he can. That may be the most excitement I have all day.

NIKKI

Blake manages to line up a meeting with Allison for Thursday. He disperses this information via text. I give it the thumbs up and respond with the single letter "k."

He's right about her inability to leave the house yet. Well, she can leave. She just can't drive or ride her bike, I guess. But hell, I'm driving a green Kia. We all have our problems! The plan is for Blake to go to her house at 1:00 PM, and Axel and I will show up around 1:20.

On Thursday, I drive the Kia to Axel's house. Trooper that he is, he looks like a million bucks. I doubt he even tried, but he's wearing perfectly fitting jeans and has a little stubble of a beard. He wears these high-dollar cowboy boots that look worn, although I know they are brand new from the photoshoot. The waistband of his boxers is slightly visible beneath the vintage fray of his navy tee. Plus, he smells like heaven. If Allison is the fan I think she is, she will pass out, or at the very least drool all over him.

Of course, Axel insists that we take his car. I'm not going to fight that. I need my "victim" to get the full movie star package and let her neighbors see his black 911 in her driveway. As we pull in, I see right away that this was the right call. The little houses on her street are packed together like puzzle pieces, only separated by the drives. Stepping out of Axel's car, I notice a few curtains pull back, and a few peeps step outside to see what the new car is bringing to their little world.

When we get to Allison's door, I feel my heart pound a little. *Shit. This has to work.* I stare absently at the spiderwebs in the corners of her windows and send a silent wish to the universe.

Blake appears at the door seconds after we ring the bell. For the first time, I see him act nervous. Mr. Composure is losing his composure in front of genuine celebrity. He isn't wearing the full suit this time and instead is wearing a pristine white Oxford button-down. The sleeves are rolled up just past his wrists. I suppose this is his attempt to look like the regular folk. He can't hide his *GQ* blonde locks or deep blue eyes though.

We step in and see the patient lying on an ugly floral couch in the front room. The house is all cheesy and full of fake plants and knickknacks—exactly what I would expect from a middle-aged bicyclist pining after movie idols half her age. Somewhere between no taste and bad taste. Wallpaper but dated. Carpet. Who has carpet anymore?

"Allison—" Blake motions to me— "you may have met Nikki Carpenter at the accident. And this is her friend Axel Miller."

Allison leans forward like she's going to get up off the couch, then realizes she can't without a lot more effort. Axel swoops in, charm at level 11 on a scale of 1 to 10. He helps Allison sit back. He even plumps the pillow behind her. The couch is covered in blankets and bed pillows. She has set up shop for the long haul.

"Are you okay?" he asks, his voice saccharine sweet.

Hell, this is Oscar worthy.

This house is seriously in need of some attention. There is crap everywhere, and I think I see a litter box in the corner. I definitely smell a litter box. I know my house is messy, but it's what I like to think of as clean-messy. I may have a few clothes laying around, but this bitch has newspapers and takeout boxes scattered everywhere. Someone needs to introduce her to a vacuum. Maybe teach her to light a candle.

"Yes, I just…" She smooths her spiky black hair down and laughs nervously. "I can't believe it's you. How? What?" She struggles to put it all together.

"Well, Nikki here is like a sister to me. She is so upset about the accident and how you've been hurt, so I had to come with her to see if there's anything I can do to help," Axel purrs. My snake charmer working his movie star magic.

"Oh." She looks at me. "I was just telling the lawyer, umm Blake, that I have to recover at home for a few days, and then I can get around on crutches. Once the cast is off, I'll go to physical therapy. I'll be all right," Allison says. She pulls at a thread on her old-lady cardigan.

Careful there. It looks like it could all unravel quickly. "All right"? That sounds pretty damn promising to me. I throw a wink Blake's way. He ignores me, keeping his focus on Allison.

"That sounds great," Axel says, taking a seat on the coffee table to get as near this nut as possible. He reaches out to hold her hand in both of his. "You know, Nikki has been *anguished* about what happened. She would never hurt a fly, and to think she caused you any pain has been unbearable to her."

Axel may be pouring it on a little thick, but Allison seems to be buying it. *Anguished?* This old girl eats it up, sap and all.

Allison looks my way, then speaks to Axel.

"I know it was an accident. Just a really bad accident," she says. Blake beams. Like he set this whole thing up! "She didn't knock me over. I did that when I flipped her…well…lost control on my own."

"When you flipped me off? I didn't even see that," I chime in. "You'd be surprised how many people do that to me. Can I get the name of your decorator?" I throw that last comment in as a little flip-off of my own.

"I know she'll be happy to pay all your medical expenses," Axel says, ignoring me, still holding her hand like they're old friends. Or mismatched lovers. I bet she wishes she'd worn makeup today. Or showered.

"Yes!" I jump in. "Whatever I can do, of course."

But Allison can't take her eyes off Mr. Hollywood to look my way. I love that he volunteers me to pay for everything, knowing that I'll most likely need to hit him up for a loan.

"That sounds good. That will be fine," Allison says.

"So you'll agree to drop any charges then?" Mr. Serious Lawyer jumps in, maybe a bit too eagerly.

Let's play it cool, Blake. You catch a squirrel by being very still with the nuts in your hand. Not by hurling the nuts at it.

Axel to the rescue. "But first, let me get a picture with you, babe." Axel coos at her, ignoring Blake.

Allison perks up even more, reaching for her iPhone.

"You do it, Nikk," Axel hands her phone to me with that sex symbol grin of his.

"And get one on my phone too please," Axel adds, handing me his iPhone as well.

"You want one of *me*?" Allison giggles, like she is a ten-year-old girl instead of a forty-five-year-old woman hyped up on pain meds.

"Of course!" Axel says. "For my socials."

Thus begins amateur photo hour with Axel and ends my hit-and-run nightmare.

Axel signs a few dozen things for her before we leave, and Allison signs a document that my handsome lawyer has brought with him, clearing me of any criminal intent or something like that. Acknowledging that this was no hit-and-run.

It's over.

Blake calls me later in the day and tells me how he worked everything out with the police department and where I can pick up my car/SUV.

With that behind us, surely he'll ask me out now.

I wait.

ALLISON

What a week. My head is spinning from everything that has happened. Axel Miller, right here in my house! After the months and months of absolutely nothing happening and time moving like molasses in my mother's assisted living facility, so much has happened in just a few days.

First the accident, of course. The bike wreck, as I think of it. The pain and the awkwardness of navigating my life with this gargantuan cast. I'm clumsy by nature, but now everything is difficult.

When it first happened, I called my dad from the hospital. I assumed the facility would be concerned when I didn't show up to visit my mother. Turns out they're oblivious to whether I show or not. She probably is too if we're being honest. My dad answered right away, certain I was calling with bad news or complaints involving my mother. No, this time it was all about me.

Dad is very helpful. He drives me back to my house after I get released from the hospital, giant cast and all. He props me up on the couch and gets me settled in.

I've been using Lyft mainly for doctor's visits and errands, but sometimes I call Dad for a ride. He never says no. It is a bitch getting around on crutches, but I do it. Thank God for Uber Eats.

Who would have thought this setback would lead to meeting my favorite movie star? He's too young for me to have a serious crush on obviously, but how could you not? After months, actually years, of spending day in and day out with the decaying and increasingly insane elderly crowd, having these young, vibrant people in my house was a godsend. Not just Axel. That lawyer was a charmer and so nice. The girl who hit me, Nikki something, was a real smart-ass. But I also liked her. She was funny. I'd like to think she's the kind of daughter I would've had if I'd had children. Or even a younger work friend if my work hadn't become all about selling carpet with crusty old men and hanging out with the elderly.

I'm aware they're all in cahoots to get me to drop the charges. But I was never going to press charges. This girl is just getting started in life. I know the heartache that lies ahead. I'm not going to be the cause of anymore for her.

I miss my bike rides and what is left of my mother. But also, I needed the break.

I have no complaints that all of this led to Axel Miller in my house.

Juno and I watch TV, both of us equally oblivious to what is on the screen. Blue tones bounce off the walls, reflected light coming from the black box.

I count my pills again.

NIKKI

I go to Bikram Yoga three times a week. It's disgusting in there. A bunch of sweaty, stinky people. Don't even get me started on the carpet. They always have carpet in the authentic Bikram studios. Some stupid thing the original guru started. According to Netflix, that guy is a racist and maybe a sexist. He's also wrong about carpet.

I usually take a hand towel and spray it with perfume so I can put it over my face and breathe when I need to. Still, nothing makes me burn calories like that workout, so I keep going.

One day, I see DK there. In my class! She tries to talk to me as I'm positioning my mat, but the whole room glares at us. There is no talking inside the yoga room. I motion for her to follow me into the lobby.

"Hey, they don't let you talk in there," I tell her.

"Oh," she says, pulling her nineties-era leotard out of her crack. "I want to see what all the fuss is about. So...what's going on with that cute guy you're seeing? The lawyer?"

Okay, so *this* is why she's here. DK wants a little outside-the-office scoop...outside the office. I rack my brain to figure out who the hell she is talking about, until it finally dawns on me that she means Blake Hoynacki. I forgot she saw me with him that first morning, when he dropped me off from jail.

"We're probably done," I tell her. True as far as our business goes, although I'm still holding out hope for a personal call. No need to fill her in on the nitty-gritty details.

"That's too bad, "she says. "I guess we should get back in there. Is it always this hot?"

I follow her in. *Great, one more place she can keep tabs on me. Is nothing sacred?*

DK lies down throughout most of the class. That pose is called "Savasana." I doubt she knows that. To her, it's probably the "when the fuck is this over?" pose. This is obviously not her thing. As the ninety minutes drone on and I'm lost in my own thoughts and preposterous poses, it seems more and more likely that the only reason she came here was to ask me about my love life. Weird.

It's two weeks later before I get it.

DANA (aka DK)

The next time Nikki is out at a meeting, I decide to snoop in her office. I don't think of it as snooping. She works for me. It's my office if you think about it. Even so, I shut the door behind me quietly. I don't turn on the lights. I sit down at Nikki's desk, which is littered with scattered magazines and notes to herself, a few bills. Post-it notes. A schedule of those awful Bikram classes. I'll never do that again.

And a date book.

She is the only twenty-something in the world who has an actual date book. I have told her countless times to schedule her appointments on the shared Google calendar. She refuses to let me keep track of her. I would fire her if it weren't for Axel Miller. He might not be the biggest name we publicize, but it's the one with the most cachet. Having him here attracts clients and gives us credibility.

It doesn't take long to find what I am looking for—the name Blake Hoynacki scribbled in Nikki's childish scrawl with a phone number. "Lawyer" written beneath his name. Or "lawme"? I can't understand her handwriting,

She's not seeing him anymore, straight from her own mouth. So what does it matter if I call him? I copy the number on to a sticky note and slip it in my pocket.

I open the door, peer down the hallway, and step out of her office. I silently shut the door behind me. The swish of my leggings and faux leather boots rubbing together gives me away.

"Good morning, Dana," Rachel says from the front desk as I try to slip past her. "Should I tell Nikki you're looking for her?" she asks not so innocently.

"I'm not looking for Nikki," I say, stopping in my tracks. This girl is as nosy as I am.

"Got it," Rachel says as she answers an incoming call.

I walk to my office and pull the phone number from my pocket.

BLAKE

I scroll through Nikki's Instagram feed for the tenth time. Nothing new posted, but I never tire of looking at the pics. And her captions. Always so dry and dead on. This is a girl who has no idea how good-looking she is. She doesn't post selfies like other girls her age do. She lets her humor lead. If only she realized how much the humor sometimes bites, but she lingers.

Weeks have passed since I last saw her, and that was just professionally. Smart girl, worming her way out of that bicycle thing. I haven't dealt much with celebrity and had serious doubts that her little scheme would work. But it did. I found the whole thing, and her, charming.

There's a bit of a paper trail to wrap up, so we have exchanged emails. I forward my invoice. Even there, she is funny. I normally pass this stuff off to Tony in my office, but I want to be the one to get her little quips.

When Dana calls, I see the company number on my caller ID and my heart jumps a little. I know it sounds ridiculous that I get excited at the thought of it, but I'm sure it's Nikki on the phone. When Dana introduces herself, I'm a little disappointed.

I think about a way to bring Nikki up, but Dana is a bit much. Sharp like a knife.

I help her through some legal questions. Advice more than anything. We set a meeting.

I miss the verbal sparring I had with Nikki. I don't really experience that with the women I date. I go through the motions with those girls, but I don't feel much of anything. They're often enamored with many things—the car, the job. I'm not sure any of them are actually interested in me.

Here I am, providing professional advice to the boss of the one girl I really do feel something for. Delaying reaching out to the actual girl.

Also, I haven't stopped thinking about her.

That reminds me, I never called Ashley back.

NIKKI

I'm coming out of Ralph's in Beverly Hills when I see Blake drive by. With fucking DK in his passenger seat! *Are you kidding me?*

I am stunned.

I text my best girlfriend, Connie, and demand that she meet me for drinks. When she sends back some crap about being on a cleanse, I simply type "911 NOW." That is our code. You have to do it when it's a 911.

When Connie walks into the bar at the Beverly Wilshire, I've already ordered my second scotch and water. Classy. Choosing this place was a stipulation for Connie. Unlike Axel, she loves to be seen.

"Scotch?" she starts right in. "The clearer the liquor, the better for you, calorie-wise and hangover-wise."

"Perfect. That's why I called you—I need your help with my alcohol consumption. Thank you for your Ted Talk," I say without missing a beat.

Connie is used to me. She laughs me off as always. She waves down our waitress and orders her made up version of a martini.

Vodka with a twist of lime and a sprinkle of Splenda. It tastes vulgar but looks nice in a glass.

"You know the lawyer who's been getting up the nerve to ask me out?" I say. "I just saw him—you are not going to believe this—with DK!" It's funny and also ridiculous now that I've said it out loud.

"This is your 911 emergency?" she asks. "When you say 'getting up the nerve to ask you out,' how long has it been since you've actually talked to him?" She is always specific like that. Always calling me out on my bullshit.

Girls can be mean. All those *Housewives* shows owe their success to that fact. We claim to support each other, but we all can be petty, competitive, and jealous. Mean. Connie isn't like that. Okay, she *is* like that. But she's on my team. Like high school, we seem to exist in these cliques, no matter how old we are.

I've only known Connie for a few years, but we understood each other right away.

We were both working the pre-show red carpet for one of those random award shows. Teen Throbs or Choice or some such made-up title, one more of the endless subcategories designed for the sole purpose of celebrity promoting and gawking. She works as a producer for one of the entertainment cable networks.

Unlike most of those harried beasts, Connie takes care of herself and counts the days until she can step in front of the camera instead of working on the sidelines. She deserves to be on the other side of the camera. She is gorgeous and smart, a rarer combination than you might think.

The first time I met Connie, she was working me to get Axel to talk to her features reporter. I was pushing her to make it short. We spoke each other's language from the beginning.

"I don't know, not *that* long," I respond. "But I assume there's some sort of attorney-client window he's waiting to have pass before he calls me. But now I realize he just has suck-ass taste!" I say, tilting back my whiskey and motioning for the waitress.

"Well, good riddance. Going out with DK marks him forever in the 'not on the market' category." Connie sips her fake martini. "How do you even know they're seeing each other anyway?"

"I guess I don't know for sure, but I saw her in his car. Not sure what else it could be."

"Maybe she hit a woman on a bicycle like you did. Maybe she got picked up for shoplifting at Kmart. Maybe they're cousins, you nut," Connie calmly muses. "Besides, he's not a doctor. There's no waiting period to ask you out."

"Regardless, he has the stink of DK on him now, so that's that. Another one bites the dust." I raise my glass in a toast. Connie raises her wannabe martini, and we drink on it.

When I was younger, I assumed my love life would continue on as it had in college. I always looked over the shoulder of whatever boy I was with to check out the next one. I was always looking for funnier, more handsome. Turns out, one day you look up and no more boys are waiting in line. At least that's what happened to me. That lawyer? A few years ago, he would've been begging to bang me. And now? Now I guess he's putting it to my boss. The cougar went in for the kill while I was playing hard to get. The lion tamer must step into the cage.

Before I can spend weeks coming up with a revenge plot, I get a call that changes everything.

CONNIE

I decide to limit myself to one drink with Nikki, even though she orders a few more. I plan to go to an early Pilates class tomorrow, and alcohol tends to make me hit the snooze button. I get a kick out of Nikki and her drama—in small doses. I'm out here killing myself to get ahead while she has this super cushy job, and yet she always finds a way to get in these crazy situations.

I would die to work with Axel. I guess the grass is greener and all of that. But I love her, and her shenanigans keep me entertained.

We met on the red carpet. She was with Axel. Enough reason right there to buddy up with her. But I genuinely liked her! I still do. So many relationships in our business are superficial at best. LA is a town of "what can you do for me?" But Nikki is different. I hope I'm different with her. I tease her about the 911s, but she comes running for me too. That's worth more to me than an interview with Axel.

NIKKI

It's 2 a.m. Instead of being asleep or passed out, as any person in their right mind would be, I'm awake and scrolling through TikTok. Searching for a crush but also watching dog tricks and conspiracy theorists. You may wonder why I'd answer a call from an unknown number in the middle of the night. Nature of the job. These calls are usually some kind of entertainment emergency that needs PR stat.

"Nicole?" the voice on the other end says. Sounds like an older guy. I have no idea who.

"This is Nikki," I correct him, sitting up in bed.

Nicole is my given name. No one calls me that though.

"Oh, right, Nikki. This is…I am a friend of your mother's. There has been an accident—" He seems to gasp between words. Or sob. "A really bad accident. And your mom, she's bad off."

I stand up. Shocked. Panicked. Funny how I can make mother jokes all day long until something actually happens to my mother. "I don't understand. Who is this? Is this some kind of prank?" I'm the one now gasping, trying to put it all together.

"No, no," the man says. "Come to Cedars. I am her friend. Her boyfriend. Her whatever. Come now!" He hangs up. I'm not kidding. He hangs up. *Boyfriend?* I'm clueless about who he is or what he is. Where is Alice?

I stumble around my bedroom, pulling on clothes and shoes. I grab my purse and race out the door. I put in my AirPods. I have to call The Perfects. I don't even have their number in my favorites. Backing out of the driveway, I scroll my contacts until I land on my brother's name. I tap his home number and wait. Of course, they still have a landline.

Mrs. Perfect picks up. This is no good. "Glenn! Is that you?"

Fuck. He's not there?

"It's me, Nikki," I say. "I need to talk to Glenn. Where is he?" I ask as I try to navigate the early-morning darkness.

"He isn't here," she says with full on exasperation, no doubt ready to end the call.

"Wait! It's an emergency. Mom has been in an accident. Where is Glenn?" I might be shouting at her.

"Not here!" She hangs up. *Damn*. Julie and I have never been close, but hanging up on me is a first.

With one hand on the wheel, I scan through Glenn's contact with the other and this time hit his cell number. It rings three times.

"Nikki?" He sounds asleep.

"Glenn! Look, you shit, where are you? Your wife just hung up on me. Mom's been in an accident." Hearing my brother's voice, I am ten again, banging on the back door for him to let me in.

"What? When? Where is she?" I think the fear in my voice surprises him as much as the news about mom.

"Cedars. Meet me there!" I sniffle a little and repeat, "Cedars. Now!" I disconnect. I pull my AirPods out and throw them in the console. I let myself have a good cry as I drive. I don't even know the situation yet. I don't know why I'm losing it. But I go ahead and get it over with.

One thing about hospitals is it's never clear where to park or where to enter. I guess I need to go in the emergency room entrance, but I can't park there. I need time to pull myself together so maybe it doesn't matter.

I find a place to park, blow my nose on an old McDonald's napkin sitting on my dash, and jog through the automatic glass doors. I go straight to the information desk and give my mother's name. The woman at the desk is clearly not as concerned as I am. To be fair, I assume she has a lifetime of life-and-death scenarios behind her. I am a virgin in hospital procedure.

She types something on the computer keyboard when I tell her my mother's name. "Still in an exam room. Room 4," she says, as if I'm ordering a coffee.

I look around, dazed, searching. Miss Disinterested points in a direction without ever looking up from her computer screen.

I walk down the hall per her finger point and see a door slightly ajar marked with a 4. I push it open just enough to poke my head in. My mother lies on what appears to be one of those body board things. Exactly like they put my *victim* on. But my mother also has on a giant neck brace keeping her head pointed straight up at the ceiling. She is super still.

She isn't alone. This guy, this man, is holding her hand. His back is to me. He does that silent heave thing, like a girl. I can see his shoulders bounce a little with the effort to hold it in. He drops her hand when I come in and coughs out, "You must be Nicole. Nikki?"

"Yes," I say, waiting for him to say who the fuck he is. I stand at the end of the bed, looking from him to my incapacitated mother.

This guy is seventy if he is a day. I am so confused. His hair, what's left of it, is trimmed buzz-cut short. Coke bottle glasses perch at the end of his nose.

My mother makes some audible noise, but it's not exactly language, at least not any I can understand. I go to the other side of her bed, opposite Mr. Stranger. I look down at her.

"Mom?" I ask, searching her face. She looks right through me.

Again she makes that weird sound.

"She's had a stroke. I don't think she can talk yet. They gave her something," the old man says. I look at him with his high-waisted sans-a-belt pants and Members Only jacket. Not an ironic version of a Members Only jacket but the real damn thing, like from the eighties.

I reach for my mother's hand, and Mr. Members Only yells, "No! That one is broken!"

Right about then, Glenn walks in. He looks half dead. His clothes are rumpled, and his hair is standing up in weird places all over his head. He clears his throat, clearly thrown by the sight of the weird old guy, me, and Mom all stretched out making that crazy sound.

"Glenn!" I call out like I'm glad to see him. For the first time in a long time, I really am. His big, athletic build seems manly and heroic in this bizarre scenario.

He comes around the bed to stand beside me. We don't hug or anything crazy like that. He too goes to touch Mom's hand, and again the old guy barks, "No! That hand is broken!"

Glenn recoils like a scolded child.

"So who exactly are you?" At least my brother cuts right to the obvious question. I've just been standing here gawking, unable to engage my usual arsenal of witty repertoire.

"Sam," the old guy says between his girly sobs. As if that name means something to us.

Nurses storm into the room. That's what it feels like to me anyway.

"Are you the family?" one short, hefty nurse with a mullet says to Glenn, handing him a clipboard. She rocks back and forth in her knock-off HOKAs.

Glenn looks at the paperwork he's just been handed.

"We need to take her into surgery. Her left arm has a severe fracture. Please sign here and here." She jabs her meaty paw at the paper.

Glenn snaps into Glenn mode and signs, smoothing the form back down and straightening it beneath the clip. He hands it back to the bear and asks, "When will we speak to a doctor?"

The nurse grabs the board back from him and tosses it to the end of my mother's bed. A band of minions emerges from the woodwork. Suddenly my mother is being rushed down the hall with the sniveling Members Only man, *Sam*, scurrying behind them all. Shorty yells over her shoulder, "Someone will speak to you before the operation."

***

Glenn and I stand there lost like the children we have become.

A new bed is rolled into the room almost immediately by a whole different set of minions. I feel weak. I want to crawl up on this new cot and shut my eyes for a minute. Instead, I sit down on the hard chair.

Yet another nurse, this one younger and kinder, says to me, "Are you okay?"

Finally!

"She's fine," Glenn says. "They just took our mother to surgery." Glenn speaks for me. Yes. Good. I am too weak to speak. I lean back and stretch my legs out.

New Nurse says nicely, "You need to go to surgical waiting then. You can't stay here."

Without turning back to look at me, Glenn is out the door. I struggle out of the chair and hurry to catch up with him at the elevator. He has already pushed the call button. The doors open before I reach him. We step inside silently.

When we get to the waiting room, the old man is in a corner, head in his hands. His heavy breathing is the only sound in the room aside from the drone of CNN coming from a TV hanging on the wall. With the rows of gray cloth attached chairs and dated magazines, this could be Jiffy Lube—except for the whimpering Sam. Although I suppose some people cry during oil changes.

Glenn and I sit opposite each other, far from Sam.

"So what's the deal with the wife?" I ask.

Without answering me, Glenn gets up and announces he's going for coffee.

I look down at my shoes and realize they don't match. Both Nikes, but one is a running shoe and one is for tennis. Really? One is white. One is not. Can my night get much worse?

Glenn returns and hands me a Styrofoam cup with a plastic lid. "I don't know what you like in it, so it's just black," he says.

"Ah, sludge. My favorite Starbucks order," I reply, taking the toxic waste from him.

He takes the seat opposite me again and says in a low, secretive tone, "Julie and I had an argument earlier. I'm sure that hangup was meant for me, not you. I apologize on her behalf." His words come out in a rush, like he tried them all in his head before spilling them out on me.

A perfectly rehearsed answer to my earlier question. I have no idea how to respond to this chink in his armor.

I rise and take the hot cup over to Sam. "Coffee?" I offer.

He looks up from his hands. His wrinkled face is pasty white, and his eyes are red. That's when I notice it. A wedding band on his left hand. I am still standing there, arm outstretched with the coffee.

"You're married?! You and my mother are married?" I blurt out.

He takes the coffee. His left hand shakes as he opens the top. It makes his ring catch the light coming from the overhead fluorescent bulbs. I don't know if the shaking is because he is upset or because of his advanced age.

"No. No. I'm married," he says. "But not to Anne." He winces a little as he mentions her name, as if his tears might start again.

"Your shoes are wrong, I think," he offers, apropos of nothing.

I huff back to my seat and give Glenn my best death stare.

A nurse or doctor or some such person of indeterminate gender walks in.

"The doctor is getting started with your mother," he/she or they says to us. "The surgery will take at least four hours. The surgeon will have to insert a metal plate in her arm and set it. We administered TPA, and that seems to have stopped the stroke, but the doctor will check to be sure. We aren't sure of the damage, long term or short term. I'll be back to keep you updated."

As he/she leaves, Glenn pipes up, "Your shoes are mismatched."

"I know. You have no sense of fashion," I counter.

We sit in silence, except for the occasional heavy sighing of Sam across the room and the hum of CNN. Erectile disfunction ads seem to rule the overnight programming.

"I think I'll run home and remedy this shoe situation. It seems to be a big problem for everyone. I'll be back soon," I say addressing no one. Neither man responds.

I retrace my steps to the elevator. Down to the lobby. I stumble in my mismatched shoes back into the early-morning darkness and search for my car.

When I'm back behind the wheel, I sit staring blankly through my dirty windshield. I don't cry. I'm more mystified than sad. So much information in the middle of the night. I turn up the radio as loud as I can to block out the noise in my head.

Back home, I throw myself across my unmade bed. I shut my eyes for what I tell myself will only be a few minutes. Thirty at the most. I kick off the offensive sneakers, and sleep overtakes me.

My dreams are fuzzy and frantic. Sam and Glenn and my mother but not in a hospital. They are at a playground in a park. My mother is on the swings. Sam and Glenn take turns pushing her from behind and then start pushing each other. I watch from the merry-go-round.

SAM

I meet Anne's children, and I'm bawling like a blubbering old man. It was never in our plans to meet each other's children. There is no need for that. We haven't ever discussed doing that. The kids are all adults. We don't talk about them much. I talk about mine more than she does hers. Even so, that life seems separate to me. Not better or worse than what I have with Anne. Just other.

My wife, Mary, and I were high school sweethearts. I always considered her the love of my life—until I met the real love of my life, Anne. One of the great ironies of life is that you start living before you even know who you are. When I was young, everyone got married early. Once you were of age, you married whoever you happened to be dating at the time. It is what you did. You got married and had a family. It's what the church and our families taught us.

I am still married to Mary. And I love her. But I am in love with Anne. This late in the game, I realize the difference.

Now Anne is in surgery, and I think I fumbled meeting her children. I am falling apart.

I pick up the remote from a side table. I push the volume button repeatedly to turn down the incessant noise of the TV. It doesn't work. I sit alone in the surgical waiting room.

GLENN

I leave the hospital soon after Nikki. I see no reason to sit here with this strange old man. I also see no reason to let Nikki know I'm leaving.

There must have been a shift change because, as I pass the information desk, a hot young guy takes a seat behind the counter. Dimples for days. I don't let my gaze linger for long. I can't afford that here. That's why I am in this thing with Julie if you think about it.

But none of this is what she thinks is going on. She is convinced I'm super busy with work or that there is another woman. But I'm not and there isn't.

There is a man.

There have been women…but also men.

When I was in high school, one of my asshole stepfathers had this son, Axel. My God, that kid was hot. All tan and lean, but muscular too. He is a big actor now. I used to wrestle around with him, but I would get hard and have to go all bully on him so he wouldn't know. But hey, I was a kid! The wind could blow wrong, and I'd get an erection. Even my sister could accidentally get me hard, but of course I never acted on it. Not with her and not with Axel.

But in college? In college, guys seemed to know if you were up for that sort of thing.

The first time, after a few beers at one of those dive bars around every college campus, this thirty-something guy told me he was leaving out the back way. We had flirted over a beer. I didn't really know it was leading anywhere, but I hoped. I had this feeling in the pit of my stomach. Anxious. Excited. Just enough alcohol in me to be open to possibilities. I followed him out a few minutes later. He grabbed me from behind before the door even fully shut. It was rough and fast. I was hooked.

I never saw that guy again. Oh, I looked. Went back to the bar alone, several times. But I didn't need to see him again. He had opened the door, and now I knew I was willing to go through it. You'd be surprised how easy it is. I hooked up at other bars. Clubs. Frat parties. Yes, those boys too. Mainly stranger encounters and one-night stands. No dating. I dated girls. Always. And my junior year I met the perfect girl, Julie.

She was in my speech class. I was average in that class, good enough but nothing special. She was so poised and articulate, even though her speeches were usually about things I cared nothing about. I asked her to help me. That's how it started with us. We would sit in her dorm room, or mine, and rehearse our speeches for class. I knew I sucked, but she always told me I was great.

"You're so relaxed and funny when it's just the two of us," Julie told me, laughing. "That's who you need to be when you give your speeches. There's no need to tense up and become a robot."

I would laugh with her, and I would try to relax. But when it came time to stand in the front of the classroom, I always stepped into the role of Serious Man, or Adult, or whatever I thought I was supposed to be. Man of the House. Ringleader.

Julie would sit at her desk and mime a big smile to try to get me to relax.

Julie was everything I wanted in a future wife. She was, and still is, beautiful. Short wavy hair the color of autumn leaves. Petite and so girly. It was easy to be the man with her, open car doors, pay for dinner. She was not only beautiful but also smart and sweet and kind, and she loved me. Really loved me. She still does as far as I know. I love her too.

This other thing? It was a hobby of sorts. Nothing to do with Julie. I would never hurt her, then or now.

When I got down on one knee a month before graduation, in the restaurant where we had our first real date, I honest to God felt like I could give it all up. I could commit to her fully. If she said yes, I thought my life would truly begin and I would put everyone else behind me.

I did for a while.

Our first year of marriage was all Julie and I both thought it should be, I think. She was the consummate wife; I was the quintessential husband. I got a good job with upward mobility. I passed the CPA exam. We bought a house with a room for a future nursery. Julie made us dinner every night. All the things my mother had never done or never had time for.

I didn't push Julie to work. She was so busy making our house and our life what we wanted that she didn't seem to have time or a desire for work anyway. I liked coming home to her and to a clean house and to dinner already on the table.

We entertained friends. People we knew from college. Men I worked with and their wives. We became experts at playing house.

Then there was a woman. Nothing special. I don't even remember her name now, if she even gave me her real name. She was a girl at a bar in a town where I was attending a seminar. My attraction to her wasn't caused by unhappiness but born more out of boredom and a shade of loneliness. Because of her and that night in my hotel room, I realized I could do these things and Julie would never have to know. It rekindled some excitement in my life that I thought had ended with college graduation and marriage vows.

Eventually I turned back to men. Much less complicated and more anonymous. The women always scared me a little with their emotions and random texts. I didn't want that. Way too much risk that Julie might find out. In my mind, I justified that I wasn't really cheating if it wasn't with a woman. And it stayed pretty much one-time encounters.

Until Tony.

I met Tony at a company softball league. My team was pretty good actually. Tony is not on my team. I would never be that stupid.

We met the first time we played Tony's law firm—well it isn't exactly his law firm. Tony is a paralegal with not much aspiration to be anything else as far as I can tell. We never talk about it.

The first time we played them, we kicked their asses. I noticed Tony right away, laughing in the dugout. Not in a queenly way. I'm definitely not into that. He seemed so comfortable in his skin and genuinely happy. Afterward, when we formed lines and slapped the others' hands in the name of good sportsmanship, Tony grabbed my hand and held it a little. A quick thing. Nothing anyone but the two of us would notice.

The next time my team played that firm, I was eager before the game. Excited like a teenager. My eyes were on Tony all night. I could hardly field a ball. At the post-game lineup, again he did the little hand grab. Now I knew it hadn't been an accident.

I was sitting on the tailgate of my truck after, changing out of my cleats and back into trainers. Tony walked by and without stopping or making eye contact said, Wanna grab a beer?"

"Sure," I responded in a decibel so low I doubted he heard it. I hurried to the driver's seat and followed Tony in his little convertible VW Beetle. He headed straight to his apartment. I followed him in, just seconds behind. He was stepping into the shower when I came into the bathroom, stripped, and followed him into the water.

That's how it is with men. No bullshit games. Right to the point. I cannot tell you how much I crave that sometimes.

Now I'm driving back to that same apartment. Not home to Julie like I should be. I can't help myself. I have already pissed Julie off for the night anyway, and I know Tony will have no questions for me. When I walk in to find him still sleeping on his stomach, comforter half-assed thrown over him, I simply take off my clothes, slip into the bed, and breathe.

Tony's alarm goes off at 7 a.m., and I'm mad at myself that I slept this long. I should already be back at the hospital, and I need to go home and change. When Tony reaches for me, I decide a few more minutes won't make things any worse.

I need this.

***

I come in the back door of the house I share with Julie. She's at the kitchen table looking like hell. She's wearing an old sweatshirt and gym shorts, not the gown and robe she usually wears for bed, or the coordinated outfit she normally has on this time of day. Her hair is pulled back in a severely tight pony, wayward ringlets still escaping around her face. In our real pretend life, she would never look like this at 7:45 a.m. We have this whole 1950s thing going on in our house, where she is up and fully dressed, making my breakfast, by the time I come downstairs. It's what she wants. What we want together. Eventually it'll be the whole family, two kids and a dog. She created a life on a Pinterest board and willed it into existence, me included. I am a willing participant in this masquerade.

I never stop moving. Just squeeze her shoulder and grab the coffee mug waiting for me on the counter.

"Mom had a stroke and fell. I've been at the hospital all night. I've got to shower and get back there," I say as I take a sip from the cup, my hands not even shaking I am so accustomed to the duality of my existence. I don't give her time to answer as I gush out the words without a breath and bound up the stairs to our master suite.

So unlike our usual mornings, the bed is a wreck and one nightstand is covered with used tissues. My side of the bed looks untouched; hers is a tangle of sheets and Kleenex.

I stand in the shower longer than usual, letting the steam and the hot water melt away my sins.

When I get out, I wrap a towel around my torso and stand in our perfectly organized closet, selecting a pair of black pants from a row of black pants. A blue shirt from a row of blue shirts. A black tie with a tiny blue pattern from a drawerful of carefully folded, identically colored ties with only slight pattern variations.

When I finally walk back to the kitchen, Julie is rinsing dishes and loading the dishwasher.

"Is she going to be okay, your mother?" She asks, not turning to look at me. With that question, I know that our life is still intact and she has forgiven me.

"I think so. I think so." I squeeze her shoulders again, kiss the top of her head, and hurry out the door to return to the sanctity of my truck.

TONY

I hear Glenn come back into the apartment. I don't look at the clock, but I know it's still late, or maybe early morning. I feel him slip into the bed, but I pretend to be asleep. Knowing he is next to me is both familiar and disturbing. I have let him become so comfortable here. Too comfortable.

I hear his breathing slow and become heavy, sure signs that he is asleep. I am awake the rest of the night. When my alarm sounds off at 7:00 a.m., I pull him to me.

ANNE

My head is killing me. I'm sure I've said those words before, but I never knew what it really meant until now. When I first open my eyes, I can feel the weight of my eyelids. I close them again.

"Anne! Anne! Did I see you open your eyes? Are you coming around? Oh, Anne!"

It's Alice. She is obviously distraught, so I force my eyes open again. I see her face leaning over me, full of questions.

I try to sit up.

"No! Lie down!" She gently pushes me back, adjusting the pillow beneath my head.

I take that as a cue to close my eyes again. Then I hear a voice I don't know.

"Anne, are you awake?"

It's a soft, soothing voice. I look up to see a woman in hospital scrubs peering down into my face from the side opposite Alice.

"I'm awake," I creak out. My throat is incredibly dry.

"Oh Anne! You can talk!" Alice exclaims and throws herself back into a chair, simultaneously scooting up next to what appears to be my bed.

"You had a little accident," the kind voice says. "You're recovering from surgery. See this button?" She gently curves my fingers around a cylinder with a button on top. "Push this if you need some pain medication, okay?"

I push the button to demonstrate that I understand and because I am in pain. I ache all over. The kind woman leaves the room.

I try to open the fingers on my other hand, the one not squeezing the pain controller. Nothing. My hand feels numb and huge all at the same time. I lift my head and look down to see a cast from my elbow to knuckles. The effort exhausts me.

"Oh, honey. Just lie back!" Alice tells me. "You don't need to lift a finger. Well, you can't lift a finger on this hand." She thumps the cast.

I do as she says and lie back on the pillow, staring at the ceiling. "What?" I ask.

"You fell, I think, and had a stroke. Or had a stroke and fell. Broke your arm. And poor Sam was there," Alice rapid fires. "He has been here all night. And your kids. I think the doctor stopped the stroke or something like that."

"My kids? *And Sam?*" I turn my head toward her, trying to piece it all together. Sam and my kids in the same room strikes me as more pressing than the news of my injuries.

"Yes, Anne. Your kids. And Sam. We're all adults here. I think it all went fine, but Glenn and Nikki were both gone when I got here. Sam called me crying so, it took me forever to understand what was going on. He's down in the cafeteria now. I told him I wouldn't move from your side until he gets back."

"But the kids know? About Sam?" I try to understand this chain of events.

"I think so. They must. He said he called Nikki and she called Glenn and they both came."

As Alice says this, Nikki walks through the door.

"Well, speak of the devil," Alice says.

"Mom!" Nikki says with more passion and genuine enthusiasm than I've heard from her since she was a little, little girl.

"Nikki," I respond hoarsely. I turn to see my all-grown-up daughter, dressed in jeans and a hooded sweatshirt. She looks more like the teenager she was just a minute ago than the young professional she is today.

"I'm okay," I manage to say, pushing the pain med button yet again.

Nikki actually touches my good arm. I can't remember when she last touched or hugged me.

"You look awful. God-awful." That's the Nikki I know. She adds in a tiny, quiet voice, "I was worried."

I cough to clear my throat from the hoarseness. And my head.

Next Glenn storms into the room. He reaches down to hug me, somehow knocking a cup of coffee from Alice's hand all down his beautiful and I'm sure expensive shirt. The hot liquid melts the garment into his skin.

"Damn, you're graceful," Nikki taunts.

"Oh, I am so sorry," Alice says, slapping the hot liquid further into Glenn's skin through the shirt, I assume in an inane effort to blot the growing stain.

He winces. He moves to the mirror to look at the mess. He peels the wet fabric away from his skin. I cringe for him.

"So much for your starched shirt," Nikki teases. She takes off her hoodie and hands it to him, revealing a Harry Styles T-shirt underneath. To everyone's surprise, Glenn loosens his tie, removes it and his shirt, and puts on the sweatshirt. The seams bulge around his arms, and the bottom is a good inch shy of the top of his pants.

We all laugh. Nervously.

"I think I'll scoot downstairs and give you all some time to catch up," Alice says, bending down to kiss my cheek. With that, I am alone with my children.

"So, Sam," I choke out in my husky voice.

"Your married prince. Such a charmer," Nikki says as she hurls herself in a huff into Alice's vacant chair.

"Nikki!" Glenn shushes her.

"So how long?" Nikki asks, ignoring her brother.

I turn to look at her, but even that hurts.

"Give her a break. She's in the hospital for Christ's sake!" Glenn scolds her.

Nikki continues to stare at me. Fists clenched. Waiting for my answer.

I turn back to look at the ceiling. "A while. A couple of years. It has nothing to do with us, with our family. It's complicated," I whisper.

Nikki stands up and leans over me, forcing eye contact. "Well, you wouldn't *believe* what we've been thinking about you and Alice all this time. Alice isn't your girlfriend?" she asks me with thinly veiled hostility.

"What?" Glenn says, shocked. "I never thought that!"

"Oh, just me then?" Nikki shrugs. "She's always around, and she is always so bossy, and I thought…" She leaves the sentence hanging there like the question it is.

"Alice has been a dear, dear friend to me. She knows Sam. I didn't want to worry you kids," I say.

It's a relief actually. Maybe the pain meds are giving me the courage I've lacked to talk to my children about my own damn life.

Just then, at the worst possible moment, but maybe the best, Sam steps into the room. The look on his face is grim, then relief. That grin of his as he looks at me…I can't help but smile back.

Nikki again slams herself back into the chair.

"Oh, Anne! You're awake! You look good!"

Sam comes over and presses his palm against my check. I relax into it, as if the kids, the monitors, the cast, none of it exists.

Glenn clears his throat. "I gotta get going. Work. Feel better, Mom. Check on you later." He grabs his shirt and tie from the sink and is gone.

Sam can't take his eyes off me.

Nikki stands up. "Good to see you again, *Sam*," she emphasizes his name as if she's talking to a child.

I close my eyes and squeeze the pain button again. I'm not sure it's intended for constant use like this or if it even works that way. Sam strokes my hair. That feels good. I can hear Nikki stomp out as I melt into his hand. She leaves without saying goodbye.

I can no longer hold my eyes open. I can smell Sam next to me. I remember the first time I laid eyes on him.

I had talked to him on the phone for months. He was one of our best clients. With multiple rental properties, he was always calling the office to purchase a new insurance policy or file a claim. Over time, we began this sort of phone flirtation that I don't think typically happens anymore. Most clients email, and texting has replaced calling. I prefer talking.

***

Sam always made me feel special, even when our conversations were all business. He was kind and thoughtful and asked about me. You'd be surprised how few people do that.

At some point, his calls became more social, more casual. He no longer asked to speak to my boss, he just chatted with me. The conversations were less and less about policies and more and more about everything else. We talked about movies and books and politics. He told me about his life. His adult daughter. He cared about my opinion.

I was falling blindly without ever having seen him in person. I knew he was married. He never hid that. I knew about his wife, Mary, and her dementia. I knew everything about him except what he looked like. I even read his insurance file like I was Nancy Drew, hungry for any information I could find about him.

One day, he asked to schedule a lunch with me. I dressed that morning like a girl going on her first date. I wore a skirt and boots and my most flattering blouse. I watched the clock like a kid on Christmas Eve. Counting the hours, minutes, until we would finally meet in person.

When he walked in the restaurant, it made no difference to me that he was short and balding and older. I felt my thighs tighten and weaken at the sight of him. I swear, when he sat down and spoke in that voice I had grown to love on the phone, he had me.

That first day after lunch, we made out in my car like high schoolers. I wanted him like I have never wanted anyone else. Not since the kids' dad died. He didn't push for more. He pulled back. Said he couldn't do this. But neither of us could wait for long. By the end of that week, we both gave in. In this old motel at the beach, in a bed that I swore was going to break. I know it sounds awful. But it wasn't awful. It was one of the loveliest things that has ever happened to me.

There was no need to tell the kids. Mine were too busy with their own lives to have any idea that I was a real person, not just their previous landlord and provider. An obligation by blood. Someone they had to check in with occasionally but never beyond the surface. Even that was a checklist of all that was happening in their lives, not questions about mine. As for Sam, he couldn't bear to break his daughter's heart.

It was easy to sneak away for lunches and stretch cocktail hours into long nights wrapped up in Sam. The secrecy only added to the attraction. It was just the two of us. And Alice. Alice was my only confidante. To her I said, "I love him."

We didn't talk about the future. I only wanted to hear his voice. Feel him next to me and inside me. I didn't dare bring up anything that would take that away from me.

NIKKI

I need to catch my breath when I leave my mother's hospital room. I lean against the wall in the hallway for a minute to pull myself together. I don't know how I'm supposed to deal with all the chaos at work like a bona fide adult and then be with those people for ten minutes and become a child again.

That way she looked at Sam... The way he looked at her. Embarrassing. Let *him* take care of her.

Alice finds me that way, still leaning against the wall.

"Nikki, honey, are you okay?" she says to me all concerned, like a real stepmother. Wait, Alice isn't my stepmother. More like Sam is my stepfather. I could use a Xanax.

"I'm fine," I say as I stand upright and pull at my faded T-shirt, stretching it beyond the top of my jeans. "Just tired. *Sam* is in there with Mom," I tell her. "I should go."

"Wait. I want to talk to you," Alice says. "I know this Sam thing may come as a surprise to you, but you need to cut your mother some slack."

"Slack? I'm here, aren't I?" I can't believe she's talking to me this way!

"You are a goddamned grown-up, Nikki. What your mother does, and frankly *who* your mother does, is none of your business! I certainly haven't seen you around holding her hand when she's needed it," Alice fires back at me.

"I thought that was your department," I snap.

Alice slaps me. Can you believe that? Not a big smack, just a little pop, but the dyke can pack a punch. She's a good half a foot shorter than I am but almost twice as wide. What I took for all fat is actually solid.

I rub my jaw and walk away. Away from Alice, away from my mother, away from Sam.

ALICE

I have been so distraught over Anne, but that is no excuse. There is no excuse. I shouldn't have slapped Nikki, but I have my reasons. That girl has been nothing but a spoiled brat for years. I can't believe the way she talks to her mother or more like *doesn't* talk to her mother most of the time.

Glenn treats Anne like a China doll, and Nikki treats her like a leper.

Anne isn't perfect, but she is neither of those things. She has been a good friend to me. Always. She is my only friend, but she doesn't hold that against me. I know I'm a lot for some people, but never for Anne.

Nikki thinks she knows, but she doesn't. I know how hard it was on Anne to raise those two kids with the love of her life dead. From suicide at that! I know the anger and perhaps guilt that compelled her to force the wrong guy into being the right one time and again. How she was let down. Beaten even by one of them. I know.

Anne told me about Sam when he was just "a nice man on the phone," and I have even met them for dinner a few times. He is a sweetheart. I'm so thankful she has him. Finally, a real prince charming, even if he doesn't come with a white horse and all the rest. Nikki doesn't yet understand that they rarely do.

Sam is so good to Anne.

I've had love in my life at times but never like this. Sam and Anne's situation may be awkward or seem wrong from the outside, but with those two, it feels like the most natural thing in the world.

So what if Anne has those two kids. That's not enough. If she was relying on Glenn and Nikki for family, she'd basically be on her own.

I'm Anne's family. Sam is her family. And I'll be damned if I let that little snotty kid, Nikki, come in here and belittle that.

ANNE

I am somewhere between consciousness and sleep when I hear Sam's phone ring. I recognize the ringtone he has set for his daughter. Like my kids, she is all grown up. More than that, she is a middle-aged woman. But she still has her father wrapped around her finger. I love that about him.

"How are you, darling?" I hear him whisper.

"No, no. You aren't bothering me. I'm in a meeting; I'll just step outside."

I hear him creak toward the door, but I don't bother to open my eyes. I still sense someone in the room.

"Anne, Anne, are you awake?"

It's Alice.

The weight of my eyelids seems unbearable, but I crack one open to see her searching my face. I try to smile, but one corner of my mouth feels heavy.

"I am afraid Nikki and I had a little fuss, so she has gone for now. But I am right here if you need anything," she says.

I close my one eye again. Ahh, Alice. Always so eager to be my everything. My protector, even from my own children. I see where

Nikki may have gotten the wrong idea after all these years. Some friendships are like that. One person more the caregiver, the other one more needy.

The door opens again, and I will both eyes open.

"Sweetheart, Ali is here, just by coincidence. She has an appointment and needs a ride home because she still can't drive. I told her I'm here visiting a friend. If it's okay with you, I'm going to run her home, and I'll come right back. Are you good?" He is so attentive to me. Always.

I nod or try to. He stoops to kiss my forehead and is gone.

"Allison is still recovering from that bicycle thing? " Alice asks, rhetorically. "I can't believe she isn't going to prosecute whoever hit her. She isn't working and is calling Sam to run her around?" Alice says for what must be the tenth time since the whole bicycle thing happened. I wish I had never told her.

I struggle to come up with an answer, but there is no answer. I know Sam. Allison comes first. His child. I fall somewhere after that, somewhere behind Mary too. But what is the use of telling Alice that that's okay with me?

This is plenty for me. Having him in my life is all I need.

NIKKI

I sit in my car a good ten minutes trying to calm down before I pull out of the hospital parking lot. That bitch slapped me!

I drive toward the office, even though your mother having a stroke seems like a good reason to skip work, a reason even DK might excuse.

My mother has been in a long-term affair—and not with Alice. My sense of reality is all distorted. I'm forced to look at my life through some new fun-house mirror. Alice is a friend. *Sam* is my mother's boyfriend.

For the first time, it's like I'm seeing my mother is an actual person, not simply an actor in the movie of my life, a bit player role I cast her in years ago. Apparently she is the lead star of some other drama I know nothing about. But Jesus, she needs help with the actors she picked. All those losers over the years and now this guy who is old and weak and *married*. And not Alice. Now that I've seen behind the curtain, I wish I could go back to being blind to it all.

A horn blares behind me, and I realize I'm sitting still at a green light. I floor the gas pedal; the transmission jumps.

SAM

I think Anne is going to be okay. But I'm not sure if I will be. There don't seem to be any lasting effects from the stroke, except that she is so tired and weak. She is still Anne. All I want to do is help her. Be near her.

Damn her kids. And my daughter. And Mary. All of that seems like nothing to worry about now. I love Anne.

She was only a voice on the phone for months. Someone who would listen to me when Mary was no longer capable of that. She was so full of life when the life I had with Mary had faded into oblivion. A friendly voice that brought daylight into what had become a dull existence. Talking to Anne was the highlight of my day. I found reasons to do it more often. She made me feel interesting. And no one found me interesting anymore.

Once we met in person, the conversations were even better. That's the extraordinary thing. We never tire of talking. We never tire of each other.

I couldn't believe in the beginning that she found a man like me attractive. I still can't believe it now if I'm being honest. I realize anyone looking at us would never understand the physical attraction. But we are soulmates.

I can never leave Mary. I know that. We are bonded by sacrament. I made vows to her, even though she has no way to hold up her end of that bargain now.

God knows.

As an altar boy, certain things were ingrained in me early on. The ritual, the symbolism. The boy that swung the chalice of incense in the processional each Sunday still lives inside of me. I take pride in all of it. It guides me. Love of family and God.

Also judgement of family and God. I believe those laws are as present and inescapable as any laws. They inform my life.

What I have with Anne may damn me to hell. But it is my willful sin. My cross. I go to church every week and, on my knees, beg for forgiveness. I plead for a way for it to all make sense. Now I also beg for Anne to be healed.

DANA (aka DK)

I never wanted to be in publicity. It wasn't my first choice. I had always liked the idea of Hollywood and glamour, but I never knew exactly how I would fit in. A small part of me wanted to be a performer of some kind. An actress maybe. Okay, maybe more than a small part of me. I used to love reading the supermarket tabloids when I was a kid. That's the life I wanted, before I knew any better. Now I see up close what fame can do to a person.

Growing up in East Tennessee, I spent my entire childhood dreaming of getting out. Of living the lives shown in those magazines. Parties and limos and champagne. Dolly Parton was my idol. I wished I was poor, like she was, so I could have my whole rags to riches story in *People* one day. We were middle class, not rich, like I knew I should be. Average, like I never wanted to be.

I shopped in the ladies' department at JCPenney and picked out what my mother called mature clothes. I liked the feel of pantyhose on my legs, while all the other girls wore knee-high socks. I teased my hair when other girls sported pigtails and dog ears.

The girls from school made fun of me. Maybe not to my face, but I knew about their whispering and laughing. I knew about the sleepovers I was never invited to. By high school, boys started noticing me. I loved their attention. Kyle was the first. I was fourteen.

He picked me up at my house and I sat right next to him on the bench seat of his truck, nowhere near the passenger door. He drove with one hand on my leg. His hand sitting there sent electricity shooting through my body. A magic that was new to me. He was barely sixteen.

"Where are we going?" I asked him as we drove through town and passed by all the usual high school hangouts, the Dairy Queen, and the video arcade.

"I'll show you." He grinned. "Somewhere special."

It was special. A big empty field where the sky seemed huge and the stars were infinite. He laid a blanket down in the bed of his truck and held me close. It never occurred to me that he didn't want to be seen with me.

I really had no idea what I was doing. Or what he was doing. I was still trying to be like Dolly, or so I thought. Dolly always said she modeled herself after the ladies of the night in her small town—

hookers is what we called them. I know now that Dolly only meant the clothes and makeup. I went a little further than that.

***

I enjoy my meeting with Blake Hoynacki. He is smart and gorgeous, but he sends me to another lawyer at another firm. He is a defense attorney, not what I need. I need a family lawyer.

NIKKI

I manage to snake my way into my office without being seen by DK or the town crier at the front desk. She must have stepped away for coffee or pee. Well, to drink coffee or—you get the idea.

I reach for my date book and see that it is already open. DK, of course. My refusal to use the Google calendar is apparently an invitation to scavenge my desk. I write in "pregnancy test" for tomorrow. I skip a week or so and write down "slash DK's tires." I'm not sure she knows she's DK.

I turn on my desktop and Google "stroke recovery." I fall down a rabbit hole of possibilities. Everything from inability to speak to total loss of mobility. It seems my mother has dodged the worst.

Next I Google Sam, my mother's lover. I found him by going to Alice's Facebook and searching her friends. I knew my mother would be too secretive to have him listed as her own friend. She hardly ever updates her Facebook anyway. But there he is on Alice's page. Sam North.

North.

I have heard that name recently. No. It couldn't be. I click on Sam's image and go to his page.

There she is. His last post. Allison North, standing with crutches and squinting into the sun. My bicycle victim.

TONY

I wake up to Glenn pressing against my back. I reach for him. I don't open my eyes, but I start to rock with him. I cannot deny him, or myself.

I have been down this road before. Married men—my addiction and my heartbreak. I suppose something in me wants the clichéd unattainable, but part of me also loves that none of these dalliances will last. They never do, although Glenn seems different. I interpret his silences to mean he loves me and is afraid to admit it. I also know it could just be silence. And avoidance. I care for him, which is my signal to end it. The thing with his mother is coming at absolutely the wrong time. I can feel him relying on me more, showing up at my apartment more, calling. Right when I'm ready to move on to something—or someone—else.

I picked Glenn. Spotted him at the softball field. He wore a wedding ring and had all the straight guy moves. My kryptonite. Straight guys. I looked at him a little too long. Gently squeezed his hand post-game. Little clues to see if he would take the bait. He did and it was amazing. But like fish and family, he is overstaying his welcome.

I can tell this is becoming about more than sex. I'm not saying that scares me, but I don't want it. When it's time for me to settle down with one man, I prefer it to be a man who knows who he is. Not a man who lives straight and loves gay. I mean, it's definitely hot for me. But thirty is coming at me like a brick wall on a racetrack, and I told myself long ago that thirty was the age for growing up.

My job at the law firm is getting intense too. Hoynacki trusts me more and more with the good stuff. Like, he let me meet with one of those corporate bozos while he was busy with some petty hit-and-run thing. He trusted me to dress the part, get the suits to sign off on paperwork. Meanwhile, he was outside the office working some bicycle wreck case.

I feel like I'm ready to step up professionally and personally. I can't be a boy toy for Glenn much longer.

JULIE

I keep rolling it around in my head that Glenn didn't come home at all last night. This is new. I'm upset about it for sure but not totally surprised.

I could blame it on the thing with his mother, but the call from Nikki came well past midnight, and he wasn't home long before that happened. Plus, he never came home or called home at all, after that call from Nikki. A mad dash this morning, in and out again.

I know there's another woman. Glenn isn't a good liar. He isn't even trying to hide it. The late nights. The way he runs to the shower the minute he comes in the door, day or night. The way he never looks at me.

What I'm trying to understand is not *why* there's another woman but why I don't care. I was awake most of the night crying. But not for Glenn. *For me.*

I have everything I thought I wanted. The husband, the house. I am a stay-at-home wife, waiting to become a stay-at-home mother. I'm so proud of my home and my life and, sometimes, my husband. I meet my girlfriends on Wednesdays for tennis. Glenn and I have cocktails and dinners with other couples on the weekends, his boss and his wife, colleagues in his office.

This is all I ever dreamed of growing up. Even in college, when other girls talked about careers, I longed to be married. To be a wife, part of a couple. My dream came true…so now what? I'm not even thirty-five years old.

Most days, I'm up and fully dressed making breakfast for Glenn before he walks down the stairs. Morning is my favorite time of day. We sit together and linger over coffee. He tells me what he has going on for the day. I encourage him, like I did back in college. Laugh with him even. Each morning feels full of hope. Afterward, when he leaves, is the prolonged quiet. Me, fully dressed and ready for the day, but the day either never seems to come or drags along. And drags. I listen to podcasts, sort the laundry, wait for Glenn. I daydream about walking out the door and never looking back.

Our house is decorated exactly like one I found in *HGTV* magazine. The pillows are perfect, the fabrics coordinated. We have the right tiles and paint colors. But none of it is for sitting or living. It is for looks. The house is never dirty enough to require much cleaning.

Now what? I never anticipated the nothingness of it all.

I follow a lady on TikTok who retired from banking after forty years. Now she makes pie crusts. An encore career doing something she loves. I tried this "perfect marriage" thing. I'd like to find my pie crusts now.

GLENN

I sit in my truck, still at the hospital. Nikki's hoodie stretches across my chest. I pull at the neckline to keep it from choking me. In truth, I don't know if it's the sweatshirt making it impossible for me to breathe or if it's my life in general. I turn up the air conditioning to see if that helps.

I can't believe I didn't go home last night. That was a first. What a stroke of luck that my mom had this episode. Well, stroke of luck for me, not for her. I guess *stroke* is a poor use of the word.

Sometimes I feel like the Robert Redford character in *The Way We Were*. My mother used to watch that movie every Christmas when I was young. I love the way Redford looks in it. I can relate to the story he writes in the college scene, where he says things always come easily to him. I'm like that. No matter how much I screw up, things always seem to work out for me. I have this whole secret life, but still have the American Dream with Julie. I'm able to keep them each in a silo. Both lives always go my way. Even when I do something so stupid, like stay out all night, something happens to excuse me. Like this thing with my mother. If I believed in guardian angels, I would say mine work overtime.

I am torn about going to work in this ridiculous sweatshirt or going home to change, which would mean facing Julie again. As I put the truck in gear, I know where I'll go, no matter where I *should* be going.

I drive to Tony's apartment.

I spot Tony's Beetle in the apartment parking lot when I pull in. Like most offices since the pandemic, his firm has as many work-from-home days as they do office days. I would let myself in if he was home or not. I like to sit in his living room alone. Inhale his life, exhale my own. Even so, I'm glad to see it is a home day for him.

I take the stairs two at a time, excited to see him. I turn the doorknob to his unit, and I'm jerked back by the interior chain on the door. I never noticed that his door had a chain. I've never seen him use it. I pull the door shut and knock. Loudly. Nothing. I rattle the knob, confused.

Tony opens the door but doesn't remove the chain. He looks through the crack. I can see enough of him to see he is shirtless and in boxers.

"Hey, let me in," I say.

He looks at me, in this ridiculous garb I have on, not even a smile. He takes a deep breath and lets out a long sigh.

"I can't. Not now."

I stand there dumbfounded. An asshole in a too-tight Barbie sweatshirt. My belly protruding above my belt. I cannot comprehend what is happening here. Then I hear it.

"Get back in here, Tony," a man's voice says.

Tony looks at me as he shuts the door.

DANA (DK)

My period didn't come for two months in a row. I didn't know why or what was happening to me. When I started throwing up every morning, I still didn't know. But my mother knew.

One afternoon I came home from school, in my skin-tight skirt and one too many buttons open on my blouse. My mom and dad were both waiting for me in the living room. They were never at home in the afternoon. I tried to avoid them by heading straight to my room.

"Dana! We need to talk," my father's voice boomed down the hallway before I could reach the sanctity of my bedroom. I walked slowly toward his voice, buttoning my blouse with one hand, still holding my books from school in the other.

My dad said they had called his younger sister, my aunt Cathy, in California. She wanted me to come there and live with her. I worshipped her from afar, and California was the land of all my fantasies. This didn't seem like punishment, but I could tell from my father's harsh delivery and my mother's stone-cold silence that it was.

My mother looked at my father. She never faced me. I want to say a tear rolled down her cheek. But it did not. I stood frozen in front of them, accepting my fate.

When I finally did go to my room, a big suitcase had been placed at the foot of my bed, where teddy bears and dolls still leaned against the pillows. My closet was basically empty. Someone, presumably my mother, had packed up my life. And left the stuffed animals behind.

I flew to California to move in with Aunt Cathy. It was my first time on a plane. My first time anywhere outside of Tennessee, other than our family vacations to Panama City Beach. Those were always car trips.

The flight attendants looked like models and were all so nice to me. I loved the little packages of nuts and the Cokes with ice they served. I poured the peanuts into my cup and watched the soda fizz around them, then felt embarrassed when I noticed no one else was doing it. Out the window, trees looked like broccoli, and the cars below seemed like Matchbox versions to me. An entire make-believe world.

When Aunt Cathy met me at baggage claim at LAX, it didn't seem glamorous at all. It felt dingy. The conveyor belt brought around my parents' beat-up old box of a suitcase and my childish flower-covered duffle bag. Everything was coated in grime and little flecks of glitter that had spilled from someone's luggage. But not enough glitter to overtake the filth.

Aunt Cathy hugged me big. I didn't know if the hug was for all I was leaving or all that was ahead. Both things overwhelmed me.

***

I call Blake Hoynacki again. The first lawyer he recommended is great. But I need different advice now.

NIKKI

"So Allison North is pretty much my stepsister," I say to Axel on the phone. I am lying on my couch, randomly scrolling socials as I talk to him on speaker.

"Wait, so the girl you had me visit, her father is dating Anne?" I can tell Axel has one ear to the phone and one ear tuned to whatever is going on in the background. It sounds like camera guys and a director loudly discussing blocking for his next scene.

"Yes! That's what I'm telling you," I yell into the phone. "Can you believe it?" I pause. "I'll call you later." I'm so annoyed by his lack of interest and don't want to explain it again.

I hang up so Axel can return to his precious movie.

I click the sound back on for Instagram and deep dive on Allison's feed. So she does have a cat. I knew it. More pics of her father, Sam. Not one picture of him makes it clear how my mother could be so enamored. He looks nothing like the plethora of stepfathers she has paraded into our lives over the years. Maybe that's the point.

Then I see it.

Allison pushing a wheelchair, an elderly woman serenely staring into the distance. That must be the wife, Allison's mother. She is disabled or elderly or both. Clearly not all there. Hell, my mother is pretty much stealing husbands from the handicapped section.

That thought lingers in my head, like a cartoon balloon with the words still hanging, when the phone rings.

"Nikki?" my mother creaks.

"Yes," I snap. "Did you expect someone else?" I can't help but pour on the sarcasm. Hospitalized or not, my mother has been deceiving me.

"I need to talk to you. Can you come by the hospital tonight?" she asks.

"If you want to talk about Sam, no need. It's your life." I sound like a petulant teenager. I'm aware of that, but I can't stop myself.

"True," she says. "It *is* my life, but this isn't about Sam. He is frankly none of your concern." My mother sounds tired, more tired than I have ever known her to be. Rightfully so, I suppose, since she's banged up and confined to a hospital bed. I never think of my mother as old. Or sick. But now that's exactly what she sounds like. She also sounds like she has had enough of my shit.

"I'll come by tonight," I answer, trying to mute some of my sarcasm.

"Make it before visiting hours end at eight o'clock. Also, I love you." My mother hangs up. I'm not sure of the last time I heard her say that. Maybe once or twice ever, when I was upset about a boy or going on a long trip. I know she loves me, but it's not the kind of thing we say out loud.

I go back to scrolling on my phone, not in any hurry to go to the hospital and have whatever conversation my mother wants to have. Not wanting to face the thought that Sam's wife is out there living in some sort of vegetative state or that I almost ran over his daughter. I wonder if my mother knows that? If Sam has put it all together? Is that what she wants to discuss?

Once I got two speeding tickets in the same week. I was still at UCLA and perpetually late for class, always in a hurry. I paid the tickets by scrapping together leftover money from the allowance my mother had given me. I assumed I could keep it all between the police department and me.

"Is there something you haven't told me?" my mother said one afternoon on the phone. I was caught totally off guard. There was a mountain of things I hadn't told her. I was in college for Christ's sake! I wasn't smart enough, though, to realize she had access to my car insurance records.

While I searched my mind for what sin she had uncovered or how much trouble I was in, she said, "No more speeding, or I'm going to have to take your car away."

I had managed to stay on the high wire.

***

Now I sit on new secrets. Still worried that I might be grounded.

I try online poker. Anything to distract me from whatever is coming. And why did my mother say she loves me?

ALLISON

I've moved on from the pain pills to straight wine. And the pain really has diminished. My leg is healing. The most I feel is an intense itching. Also intense boredom. I had no idea how much those hours with my mother were such a great distraction—a distraction from *me*. Sitting in my thoughts and what has become of my so-called life without the excuse of caring for my mother.

I am drowning.

More than the cast weighs me down. Every day I think, *Tomorrow I'll call an Uber and go visit Mom*. I can get around pretty well on the crutches. But why would I?

My dad stops by most days. Checks the litter box, takes out the trash, and brings me random groceries. I have become yet another person for him to feel guilty about.

He has no idea that I'm the one who feels the most guilt. Guilty over this passive life I have fallen into. He isn't to blame for that. Neither is my mother. Or that Nikki girl that ran me over.

That leaves only me.

ANNE

I hang up the phone call from Nikki and turn my head to look out the window. The end of another long day of sunshine, like always in Los Angeles. It's one of the reasons I moved here. Also for a man, but the weather was definitely a draw. I have come to dread never-ending sun and yearn for rain. There is some element of the movie *Groundhog Day* in the incessant repetition of seventy-degree days without storms.

I am thankfully alone for once. Sam is somewhere tending to Allison, and Alice left earlier.

I was also alone when the doctor came to talk to me. He sat on the edge of the bed and looked at me for a good twenty seconds before he spoke. I knew that wasn't normal. I waited for whatever he had to say.

"I am sorry to tell you this, Anne," he said. "We ran several scans to make sure we had stopped the stroke damage, and unfortunately we found a tumor. Tumors actually, in multiple places. We don't know the primary origin yet. The stroke, it turns out, was very fortunate. Fortunate in that it has given you time. Time to work out your affairs. Time to talk to your family."

I was so confused. What? Cancer?

I felt out of my body, like I was watching this scene play out from afar. But it was me he was talking about me. Me.

The doctor looked directly at me. "We can do whatever you want here. Let's keep you another night and monitor your recovery. I'll be by in the morning and we can discuss options then. I can submit you for clinical trials if you want, once we know more The most important thing right now is to take care of yourself and to help you feel as well as possible."

It was like he was talking about someone else. I could see a little saliva bubble at the corner of his mouth. I stared at that and tried to tune out his words. Both things seemed absurd, both the bubble and what he was saying. The bubble eventually burst.

Your life, my life, humming along, and in the blink of an eye—a stupid fall, a stroke, cancer. I am only fifty-three years old.

I couldn't ask him about time. I couldn't ask him anything really. He let go of my hand. I nodded, then dropped my head back to my pillow and closed my eyes. I wanted him to think I was asleep so he would leave.

He did.

That was an hour ago. I didn't sleep, of course. I can't. I am stupefied. I cannot process this new information. My death sentence.

I called my children. Glenn first and then Nikki. Hopefully they show up together. Sam has already worked it out with the nurses that he can stay the night in the plastic vinyl recliner. He likes to watch me sleep. He won't come until eight o'clock. The kids should be gone by then, and I will tell him. My sweet Sam.

Dating an older man, an older married man, it always seemed inevitable that he would go first. Either into senility or back to his wife or to the grave. Now I have to tell him that, no, it's me who will be going first. Soon. I know loss like that, and I hate that I will be that for him.

Glenn comes in, his arms folded across his chest. Always withholding, always creating a barrier. He was the man of the house way too young. I don't think I forced that on him, but did I? He wanted to be that, right? It was a way to make him feel important when his dad died. Something you say to boys, but mine took it to heart and holds on to it still. My head hurts thinking about this.

"How are you feeling, Mom?" he asks.

"Tired. Mainly just tired," I tell him and close my eyes a little longer. I *am* tired. But also I'm not ready to start this yet. This man-child of mine that I never really knew. What is he hiding behind that tough exterior?

"You said you want to talk?" he asks, sliding into the recliner from the sound of it and, I hope, finally dropping his arms.

"Let's wait for your sister," I reply without opening my eyes.

"Here she is," Glenn says.

I open my eyes to see Nikki standing in the doorway. She still looks like a young girl to me. My baby. But I know she isn't. Unlike Glenn, there is no need to guess with Nikki. She wears her emotions on her sleeve—and often carries a bat.

"Good, you're both here." I push the recline, or rather raise, button on my hospital bed, cranking myself up to a more seated position.

Nikki plops down on the corner of my bed. I cringe as the movement sends a tingle through my body.

"Jesus, Nikki," Glenn barks from his chair. "Why don't you just jump up and down on the bed?"

Nikki throws him a look and leans back on one elbow, peering up at me from somewhere near my feet. I struggle to see her over the cast on my arm.

"Listen. Both of you…" I start. "I'm going to stay here another night and get some rest." I push against the weight of my eyelids.

"Cool. Not sure why you circled the wagons to tell us that," Nikki says.

I close my eyes again. The effort to keep them open is monumental.

"There's more," I continue. "It seems like the stroke and the tests have opened a Pandora's box. More medical issues. Cancer." I look at them both.

Glenn's jaw clenches. Nikki's drops open.

"Seriously?" she says, jumping up from the bed and jarring my body all over again.

Glenn leans forward and reaches out to touch my shoulder. "Mom," he says, softly. I see his carefully constructed wall begin to crumble. The little boy I remember, the little boy who wants nothing more than to please me, sits in the chair.

"It's really a silver lining," I tell my children. "This gives us a chance to talk about what needs to happen."

"Like treatment, right?" Nikki asks.

"Maybe. There's a possible trial. But also selling the house. What to do about my affairs, as the doctor said." I struggle to get the right words out while also fighting my eyelids. I should have cut back on the pain meds before this conversation.

"Sam," Nikki growls, then immediately takes it back. "Sorry, Mom," she whispers. "I'm sorry, but what do you mean?"

I look at her. "Nikki, I need you to manage this. Get with your brother and find a good estate attorney. I need you to be my executor and to help me." The words spill out, and I ignore her unnecessary comment about Sam.

"What?" Now it's Glenn's turn to stand. And yell.

"I've thought about it," I tell my son. "Nikki is perfectly capable. You have Julie. Nikki has the time. She can do it."

"I can do it, Mom." Nikki turns to the window. She thinks I don't see her fear. I do. I also see her. The adult buried in that snarky facade.

I close my eyes again, pushing the medication button. I drift off into the darkness, feeling lighter.

NIKKI

I stare out the hospital window a long time. There is nothing to see. A sad little courtyard with empty benches. A lone palm tree. Regaining myself, I can feel my brother's hostility from across the room. Mom starts lightly snoring.

With as much composure as I can muster under the weight of this new information, I turn to face Glenn. He stands, arms crossed, watching Mom. I see something new there. He's scared.

We walk out of the room together, and I slowly shut the door. We walk silently to the smaller waiting area at the end of the hall and both sit.

"Luckily, I recently had to engage a good lawyer for my own legal shit, so I think I can track down an attorney, no problem," I say.

Glenn considers this.

"She obviously isn't thinking straight," my brother says, I assume to me, but he's staring at the TV screen. It's not even on. "I am the one who can sort everything. You're busy walking red carpets and…and…" He chokes. I've never seen Glenn so lost for words. I've never seen him gutted. Who would have thought I'd be the one who could handle a family crisis? Then again, what is PR but crisis management?

"Glenn," I reach out to touch his arm. "It's just stuff. I can handle stuff. It's Mom that's hard for me. You are her rock. She needs you."

My perfect brother bends over and sobs into his hands.

GLENN

Once again, I sit behind the wheel in the hospital parking lot. I am unable to turn the key. I cannot get control of my emotions. I am shaking. Literally shaking. It started in the waiting room with Nikki of all people. I hate that I broke down in front of her.

It is my mom for sure. And Tony. And Julie. All of it. For the first time in my life, I feel totally out of my comfort zone. No control over any of it. The tears, from years and years of holding it together, are endless. A dam has broken. When I finally stop, I am exhausted. Spent.

The night I decided to propose to Julie, I cried like this. I held the little velvet box in my hand, turning it over and over. I sat on the edge of my dorm room bed, navy blue comforter, hospital corners tucked in neatly, tears running down my cheeks. I held the little black box in my hand, thinking to myself, *You can do this. This is the right thing to do.*

"Glenn! I thought you had a date." Rusty, my jovial roommate, bolted through the door and threw himself on his bed. He reeked of beer and nonchalance. His bed was a jumble of dirty sheets topped with a stained quilt.

I snapped out of my stupor and manned up.

"I do," I told him, jumping up and out the door before he could see my face. I walked down the hallway into my future.

***

For the first time in a long time, I turn toward home. Willingly. Hopefully.

ANNE

I open my eyes sometime around midnight. A nurse is checking my vitals. She seems not to care if I participate in the process. I see Sam in the recliner. I look at his face. That face I love so much. I'm glad he's sleeping. One more night he can go without knowing.

I have already decided I'm not going through with treatment, no matter what the options are. I don't want to put myself, or anyone around me, through that. Killing the cancer would come close to killing me or might actually kill me. It is a gamble either way. The last thing I want to leave these people I love with is *me*, not struggling and suffering. Not fighting. I will spare them the pain of watching me die with the false hope that I can beat it. The doctor said tumors, not tumor. It's everywhere.

I worry about my kids, but I also know they'll be okay. They have their lives in motion. Our paths rarely intersect anymore. But Sam? I am Sam's world. Or at least a big part of it. I know Allison will take care of him, but I hate to put my precious Sam through this. I fall back asleep to the rhythm of his breathing, a comforting sound that feels like home to me.

JULIE

I'm sitting at the kitchen table when Glenn walks in the door. I didn't expect him back this early, or at all. He called me from the office to say he was going to the hospital after work. That was hours ago. He stands at the closed door, his hand still on the knob.

I cross the room and hug him, something I haven't done in so long. His body shakes with emotion, but I can't seem to muster up a tear. This feels like so much more than his mother.

He lets go of the door handle and slides to the floor. He still holds onto me like a lost child, arms around my legs. I run my fingers through his hair and pull his face to look up at me. I want to feel something.

"What is it? Is your mom going to be okay?" I ask him with more kindness than I knew I had for him.

He shakes his head. "It's worse than we thought. More than a stroke. But that's not it." And then he cries some more.

I pull away from him and go to the liquor cabinet to pull out the good bourbon. He needs a drink. I need a drink. I grab two crystal highballs and walk back to the kitchen table. These glasses were a wedding gift we never used. We registered for them together.

Baccarat crystal. I remember going through the department store with our little scan gun, picking out all the things we wanted for gifts. The glasses seemed extravagant, but I convinced Glenn we would use them. I envisioned a life where we would. They have been in the cabinet, waiting for an occasion. This wasn't the one I wished for, but it feels like the right time.

I set the glasses on the table and serve us each a generous pour from the whiskey bottle. Glenn pulls himself up from the floor and joins me at the table. He downs his drink in one swift motion.

"My mother has cancer," he says. "They found it during all the tests from her fall and the stroke. They have done scans and blood work. There may be treatment, but right now it doesn't look good."

I take a sip of my own drink and nod, waiting for the rest. I spin the glass to watch how it reflects the light coming from the overhead chandelier. It elevates the drink. We should have used these more often.

"I'm going to do what I can for her. She wants Nikki to take care of her business things. The house and whatever money there is." He looks at the empty glass.

I reach for the bourbon. I refill his glass, fuller this time. He takes a sip. I doubt he has noticed that the crystal is special.

"Nikki?" I say. "I don't get that. Do you?" I've never been a fan of Glenn's sister. She has always been so immature and silly in my mind. She's only a few years younger than we are, but I think of her as a child. No husband, not even a boyfriend that I know of.

"Mom said something about me being busy and married," he says. "It doesn't really matter." He looks at me finally. "Am I still married? Do I have a wife, Julie?"

"What do you mean?" I respond. I feel my blood slow. My heartbeat echoes in my ears. He has opened the door I thought only I knew was shut.

"I haven't been the husband you want or deserve. I know that. I have been here but not here." He turns the glass up, again avoiding my eyes.

"I guess I gave up on that long ago," I say. "You here but not here." I stare at his hands wrapped around the highball. I love his fingers. I love the wedding band we picked out together. I love the color of his skin. I wish all these things added up to more.

"Don't leave me," he pleads. His voice cracks a little. He looks at me and his eyes seem to have reverted to the eyes I knew long ago. The eyes of the boy who loved me. The eyes that looked up at me from one knee on the floor of "our" restaurant.

"I don't intend to leave, Glenn. I feel like you already left," I say. "But I'm not leaving. Where would I go?" I smile at him.

"I am back." Glenn's shaking hands grab mine, and he looks at me, really looks at me.

"I..." he starts what I can only assume is a confession. An admittance of guilt that will only make him feel better and me feel worse.

I interrupt him.

"You are back, Glenn. That is all that matters." I pull him to me.

SAM

I sit in the chapel at the hospital. Anne thinks I've gone to get something to eat, but I can't eat. Alice is with her. It is nice that women have friends like that. Men are not good at friendships, or at least I'm not good at them.

I have friends I play golf with. Husbands of couples that Mary and I used to have dinner with or lunch at the club. I never tell them anything intimate, nor do they discuss their affairs with me. We play games. We make toasts. We smoke cigars. We slap each other on the back.

I tell my priest most things, but not this. We are friendly in a church way. He counts on me to seat people in mass, to pass the collection baskets. I talk to him about Mary, both Jesus' mother and my wife. I talk to him about my daughter. I am unable to let him see that I am more human than he imagines from these small details.

I don't have anyone I could call and say, "My girlfriend is dying." *Girlfriend*. Like that is something a man my age should even have. A married man. I worry about Allison. All that time she has spent caring for her mother while I have been carrying on with another woman.

Here, alone, I cry out to God to save Anne.

NIKKI

I call Blake Hoynacki from my office. I'm at work. On time for a change. There's nothing like your mother dying to straighten up your habits, like showing up to work on time.

"Nikki," he says, not too enthusiastically if I'm honest.

"Blake," I respond with equal excitement.

"I need an estate attorney," I continue. "My mom is dying."

There is a long pause on the line.

"Interesting how both you and your boss reach out to me for any and all legal needs," he says. "I'm sorry to hear about your mother."

I am stunned. Legal needs? DK?

"I'm not sure what you're talking about, but can you help me?" I ask. I'm trying to use my least sarcastic tone, which isn't like me.

"Yes. I know someone. I'll text you the number. And Nikki—?" he says, maybe sensing that my breath is shallow, that I am in over my head—

"I *am* sorry." He says and ends the call.

I wonder what he means about DK. Legal needs? What? Why him? Well, I know why him. She can sniff out a guy attached to me or any girl in the office.

Immediately his text comes through with the contact information for an estate attorney. I'll call this guy. Maybe tomorrow. I set the phone down and put my head on the desk. On my arms like a kid in school. Which is how I feel.

BLAKE

I wonder if she notices how I answer her calls on the first ring? *Too eager*, I always tell myself afterward. But when her name pops up on my caller ID, it's like I have manifested her call. I can't stop thinking about her. She is so unlike the other girls I date. Other girls. I've never even been on a date with this woman! I stare out the window again, the whiteness of my office glaring back at me from the glass. I think of her like girls I date. Interesting.

I try to play it cool with her on the phone, prepared for our usual sarcastic banter. But when she tells me about her mother, I melt a little. I hear the need in her voice.

Ashley sends me a few unwanted texts. I finally respond.

"Checking on you. Maybe you're out of town?" the first one says. I ignore it.

A few days later, "Have you seen the new mafia documentary on Netflix? Let's get together and watch."

I finally respond, "I'm so sorry. I don't want to mislead you. I'm seeing someone."

It's a lie for now. But I hope to one day make it true.

GLENN

I wake up before Julie. I slide out of the bed as quietly as possible, grab my robe, and head downstairs.

I slept last night. Really slept for a change. I wanted to tell Julie everything, but also I didn't want to. She already thought so little of me these last few years. I dreaded putting out whatever tiny flame remained. But when she said she didn't want to hear it, I was relieved of the need to share.

I rummage through the fridge for eggs and milk and bread. I'm going to make her French toast, like I used to when we were dating. Like I haven't in years. I think of Tony. I would sometimes make French toast for him. Or pancakes. With him, there was never any chance of him getting up before me and making breakfast. There was no morning routine. It was midday or late night.

Now everything will be different. That life is behind me. This is my new start. I feel cleansed from all the tears and from the nice, comfortable lovemaking with Julie. And then I remember.

My mother is dying, and there is nothing I can do. Nothing she wants me to do. It feels like all the work is falling to my sister, but maybe I can talk to the doctors. There have to be options. All kinds of progress is being made in medical research. I can look into that. I can do that. I whisk the eggs a bit harder than necessary.

Julie comes into the kitchen, surprised I'm sure to see me at the stove. She goes to the pantry to get the coffee pods and smiles at me. I continue to cook.

DANA (DK)

Aunt Cathy was a publicist. That's why she lived in LA. It wasn't just her job; it was her life. Her apartment wasn't the chic, luxurious Hollywood Hills home I had imagined back in Tennessee. It was a random unit in a complex of random units in the valley. My bedroom was her home office, a room full of stacked magazines and press clippings, with a huge desk and a tiny futon. I lived in that room for the next five years.

My first week in Los Angeles, Aunt Cathy made an appointment for me in a strip mall not far from her apartment. The door was tinted glass, too dark to see what happened inside or who was inside. "Dr. Regina Bailey" was etched into the glass. That name still pops up in my mind sometimes.

Aunt Cathy went in with me. Held my hand in the dingy brown waiting room, but also in the cold, sterile procedure room. I lay on my back looking at the acoustical tiles that made up the ceiling and counted the squares. I remembered laying in the back of Kyle's truck, counting the stars.

I had no connection to what was happening to me. No world in which this was about a baby. This was just a mistake that was being corrected. A terrible mistake. Torn pantyhose sprayed with hair spray, a ripped skirt sewn together with a patch. When the thing actually happened, I tensed up. My aunt squeezed my hand.

And then it was over. The life I had lived. Tennessee. Kyle. It was all behind me.

I finished high school in Los Angeles in two more years, instead of the three it took for most girls my age. I had no friends. My southern loose-girl style never meshed with the California cool of my classmates. They were all tan and makeup free, and I caked on the makeup every morning like the disguise it was. The boys, well, there was always a boy. They dated those hippy girls, but I was the one they snuck out with at night. Aunt Cathy never noticed or never mentioned it if she did. Like I said, her work was her life. I was a roommate.

I started working in Aunt Cathy's office afternoons after school, and as soon as I finished high school, full time. At first it was emptying wastebaskets, and then it was filing, and then it was answering phones. I worked my way up. Aunt Cathy insisted I start community college as soon as my high school diploma was secured.

My parents? They sent me a check for graduation. They called every Sunday. I'm sure they sent Cathy money for room and board, but they never asked me to come home. They never made a trip out west to see me. And they never asked what happened to the baby. Once I was on my own, the Sunday calls stopped. I let go of a baby I never knew. They aborted a child they never loved.

***

I look at the agency's bank account online. Smacking Nicorette. I should really get one of those vape pens. The cold turkey thing does not work for me. I have transferred my cigarette addiction to an addiction to this gum.

Blake Hoynacki told me all the considerations if I was going to sell. I need to determine the value, not only in the current statements, but in future revenue streams. The Axel Miller account is a big asset. His name will bring in new clients. He is the cool factor. But a lot of solid accounts will continue on here even with me gone. If I'm honest, I am not sure which clients, if any, are here because of me. I'm pretty sure they'd stay whether I was here or not. Some older ones I inherited from Cathy. Those are the legacy clients. We also have hipper rising stars brought in by the younger people I hired.

I need to sort all of this out before I reach out to the attorney Blake recommended. I wish it could be Blake. He is so handsome and professional. I tricked him into picking me up the day we met. Said my car was in the shop, or whatever. Sitting in his passenger seat, I imagined what it would be like to ride shotgun with him on a real date. He was obviously younger than me, but age never stopped me. I could see a snag in my pantyhose where they poked out of my short dress. The clear nail polish I had applied to the hole that morning to stop the run had stuck the hole to my leg. I wondered if he saw it too. He never asked me out, and for once, I didn't push.

Who will buy this place? That's the question I keep asking myself. The girls that work in my office tolerate me and suck up to me because this is my company. Aunt Cathy signed it over to me in her will, I'm sure never thinking she'd die so young. A heart attack, unexpected and sudden, brought on by lifestyle and stress but also genetics. That is always a dark cloud on the horizon for me.

The day she died, I sat with her in the hospital alone. The room was filled with huge floral arrangements from celebrities she had worked with. Notes of gratitude and love. But no one came. The objects of her affection never left their movie shoots or touring schedules or vacations to spend time with her as the end approached. She had made them her life. But that was a one-way street.

I sat there watching the space between her breaths grow longer and longer.

When Cathy left the agency to me, I never considered selling. I loved the company. What a gift. It was a way to carry on her life's work. But now I find myself wondering, *What is my life's work?* This ain't it. Even if it was, no one in my life would give a shit about carrying on my legacy.

ANNE

When I tell Sam, it goes better than I imagined. Upsetting for sure, but it was also very tender. As always, everything is sweet with Sam.

"I will be here with you, Anne, through it all. I will do my best to make sure you aren't in pain," he said. "I wish I could take all of this from you. But you know I believe, Anne, that this is your chance to be with the kids' daddy again. I know you loved him. It's also a chance for you to be with God."

"The kids' dad?" I ask. "Do you believe he's in heaven after what happened? After what he did?" I ask Sam the question that always makes me question religion altogether.

"We all sin. He was a young man and foolish. I believe God forgives such things. Jesus told the thief on the cross next to him, 'Today you will join me in paradise,'" Sam says. "This life is barely a blip. And I will be with you soon too." He held my hands tightly. "I love you, Anne."

I wish I believed everything he believes. Seeing his faith, I almost do. I will miss him.

Alice? Now that is another story. She refuses to believe the diagnosis and wants to fix it. She wants to save me. But I don't want to be saved.

Alice and Sam are both here to take me home. He is kind with her, as he is with everyone. She can't stop crying. She tries to hide it from me. Her tears fall silently. She herself is quiet for a change. I am touched by her love for me.

I ease myself into the mandatory wheelchair, and Sam places a pillow under my broken arm. It's awkward to balance the bulky bed pillow under the weight of my cast on the narrow armrest of the wheelchair, but I do my best for Sam. He carries the few things I have in a bag over his shoulder and holds my good hand. Alice pushes me down the hallway and into the last chapter of my life.

ALICE

I manage to push the wheelchair by bumping Sam out of the way. He wants to walk alongside her and hold her hand anyway. I want that for her too. All the love she deserves for as long as she can.

Anne is like my own child, even though we're practically the same age. She is so frail. Not only just because she's sick. She has always seemed frail to me. I never had children, but I imagine the love I feel for Anne is much like I would feel for a daughter if I'd ever had one. She always comes to me for advice. She needs me to tell her what to do about those two asshole kids of hers. She needs me to manage this whole Sam situation. And now she needs me to nurse her through this illness.

And I need her needing me.

JULIE

I can't believe Glenn makes breakfast. Maybe this is the start of something new. I sit at the table and watch him absolutely wreck my kitchen. I see strings of egg white, splashed from the bowl from his aggressive whisking. Syrup has dripped its sticky fluid on to the countertop. The brown goo soaks into the porous stone.

His eagerness is palpable. I'm not sure I trust it. I can't imagine enjoying the food. All I see is the mess he has made.

"I think I'm going to go on a little trip," I say, as much a surprise to me as it is to him. "You need to spend time with your mother, and I'd like a chance to regroup."

Regroup? Who am I?

I'm not sure where this new voice is coming from, but it continues to pour from me. "We both need a break," I add.

Glenn turns from the stove and looks at me with his jaw dropped in silence.

With that, I get up from the table and walk back to our bedroom, on a mission to pack a bag and get out of this house. To where, I'm not sure. Somewhere that isn't here. I feel an interior shift. Something I haven't felt in a long time, the absence of this weight bearing down on my chest. This isn't about Glenn or about mourning my marriage. It's about me. The possibility of me, whatever that is.

I meant it last night when I said I wasn't leaving. The obligatory sex afterward was nice and yet not enough. His tears seemed to release him from his guilt, but they also freed me. I cannot imagine spending one more day in this house, dreading him not coming home. Or dreading him coming home.

I smile as I zip the Tumi shut. I have never used my suitcase, but Glenn's matching version has seen a lot of wear and tear. Business trips, so he always says. Another misguided wedding gift.

I don't notice Glenn watching me from the bedroom doorway, spatula still in hand, completely stunned, until I'm done packing. I kiss him on the cheek as I step past him on my way out.

SAM

I know now God's answer to my months of confessing.

My punishment is losing Anne. I am forgiven, but I am condemned. Life without her will be the price I pay for loving her. I dread it, but I also accept it. What we have is worth it to me. She is worth whatever penalty awaits me.

I haven't been to see Mary in weeks. But I am with Anne every day. I will face whatever comes, but for now I will love her. As long as I'm able and she'll let me, I will love her. God has given me this much.

I decide to ask a favor from my priest. I approach him after a Saturday night mass. He stands alone outside the church, lingering after all the parishioners have left. He is younger than I am but wiser I feel. He lives to serve, while I have given in to my baser desires. Yet I continue to believe that love exists in both places, as does God.

"Father Dexter, I have a work associate who is suffering from cancer. Dying. I am concerned for her soul. Would you be willing to visit her?" I ask him as we stand on the sidewalk outside the church, watching the sun give way to the night.

"Is she Catholic?" he asks.

"I believe we all are, right?" I say to him. "That's the whole point."

"I suppose you're correct, Sam," he replies kindly. "But not everyone welcomes it. Will your friend be happy to see me?" He asks, perhaps not of me, but I answer him.

"She will be grateful," I say, hoping she will.

I choose a day when I know Nikki will be at work. I ask Alice to run an errand, ensuring that Anne and I can have a moment alone before the Father arrives. I don't intend to be secretive, but I'm not sure if Nikki would agree to this. I know she'd make it a joke in some way, and it's not a joke to me. I want it for Anne; I need it for me.

"Anne, I'd like to do something for you," I tell her. I sit on the edge of the couch, caressing her face with a cool washcloth. She is so small now, and her face feels papery thin, like I might accidentally scratch it with the washcloth.

"Will you allow my priest to come in and say a few words for you?" I beg her.

Begging is not necessary.

"I'll do anything for you, Sam," she whispers.

To his credit, if Father Dexter is surprised by the proximity of death, or by the affection I obviously have for her, he doesn't show it. He acts as if this scenario is common for him, and maybe it is.

He sprinkles holy water on Anne's head and says, "I baptize you in the name of the Father and of the Son and of the Holy Spirit."

She closes her eyes. For a moment, I fear maybe she is asleep. But she isn't. She thanks him in her whispery voice.

My heart is full. This is all I want, all I feel I can ask, of God—some guarantee that Anne can move into the afterlife peacefully.

Father Dexter pulls a small book from his pocket and begins the series of prayers comprising the last rites.

Anne listens, respectfully.

ANNE

I don't feel sick. I feel tired. I spend my days moving from the sofa to my bed. Alice comes by most days and brings soup or a casserole. She even warms them and serves them to me. At first, I attempt sitting at the table with her, but I soon give into my overwhelming desire to lie down. To rest. After a lifetime, you rest. I am only good for a few bites anyway. My whole life I've felt a hunger for food, for men, for life, for all the things. Now, nothing. Even though I'm still young, nothing. The effort to eat, chew, swallow, is monumental.

Alice doesn't mind. She just wants to do for me. Laundry. Dusting. I let her. When I'm on the sofa, she changes the sheets on my bed. When I'm in bed, she fluffs the pillows on the couch. Her efforts to sustain me are kind but anxiety ridden. That, too, makes me tired.

Sam comes and sits in silence. With him, I am silent too. That is nice.

The priest is kind, and his prayers are comforting. At least for Sam, and his comfort is what I need. I hope he sees that I want to believe it for him. For us. For me. I let the water trickle down my forehead, not sure that I fully feel the holiness of it all. But I see the peace on Sam's face.

    That makes me whole.

GLENN

My world breaks into little pieces. No Tony. No Julie. She left me just like he did. Well, not just like him, but the result is the same.

Like my father did.

I push it all away. Keep the house tidy. Focus on work. Spend time with Mom. I find articles that will help her. I scour recipes and order ingredients online to concoct healing meals.

The guy at the dry cleaners asks, "Where's Julie? I haven't seen her in a while."

"Helping my mom. She's ill," I lie to him. Not about my mom but the Julie part.

I take the starched white shirts from him. At home, I remove them from the wire hangers, and hang them on the wooden ones in my closet. I make sure they're lined up correctly with the other shirts.

I throw out the plastic coverings and wire hangers. I scrub the kitchen counters. I take out the trash.

I talk with a doctor in Mexico who may have the cure we need, but I am unable to convince Nikki. Or my mother. They won't go.

I keep searching.

NIKKI

What is that saying, the days are long, but the years fly by? Each day feels like a year. I watch my mother fade away over long, agonizing days that become weeks that become months.

I sit on the floor beside her couch, and she tells me things. First in a scratchy, husky voice and later in a whisper. Her voice grows weaker as time goes by, and I sit closer and closer to her to take it all in. To take her all in.

She tells me about being a young girl and all her dreams from then. How she longed to go to college and travel. She tells me what it was like to be a young mother. To rush into marriage because she was pregnant with Glenn. I never knew that.

She tells me about being in love with my father and then losing him. She finally tells me how he drove out to the country early one morning before work with a pistol they kept in a nightstand drawer.

"We were happy," she tells me. "It was just a bad few days. He lost his job and panicked that he couldn't take care of us. We were so young." She sighed. "We could have figured it out, if only he had given me a chance."

All the things they planned to do together…that she was then forced to face alone. Silly things like visit the Grand Canyon and big things like graduations and weddings for Glenn and me. The resentment and anger that came with the loss, long before the acceptance. The ways she tried to fill the void.

I don't mind Sam anymore. He sits across the room from the sofa in my mother's old club chair. Sometimes he listens, sometimes he dozes. He only wants to be in her presence. Imagine. A love like that. I can't really. But I'm glad she has it in the end.

I have come to like him, or at least understand him. His loyalty to his wife, compromised only by his love for my mother, is heart-wrenching. Mary, his wife, has been living in a state of dementia for so long that she bears little resemblance to the woman he married. Yet he stays. For Mary and for their only child, Allison. I never tell him my connection to her. If he knows, he never says. Or he allows me the mistake.

When we begin hospice, Mom's caretakers are two feisty ladies in scrubs and cheap sneakers. I always imagined hospice to be a very formal, sterile thing (if I imagined it at all). Lucy and Stacy, the two hospice nurses, are the furthest thing from formal you can imagine.

They roll in with magic morphine lotion and "only if needed" tablets. They inventory anything left behind daily and have me sign off every day, agreeing to what is left behind, super careful to be sure I'm not sliding a little oxy or whatever my way. As if.

I'm not that far removed from the girl who would have considered that, but I can't remember the last time I had a Xanax at this point. My life now is all work and spending time with my mother. No time for anything else.

DK shockingly lets me work remotely as much as possible. She surprises me one day by showing up at my mother's door.

"I don't want to come in," she says when I answer. I am wearing boyish sweats and no makeup. My hair is in a messy bun. Literally everything she would never be.

"I brought this for you and your family." She hands me a grocery deli tray.

She also hands over a worn-out paperback, *A Grief Observed*.

"This was a big help to me when my aunt died. I lost my mother and father a long time ago," she says, standing there on my mother's stoop in her skimpy cheap dress.

Lucy calls my mother "doll." "Hey, Doll. Let's sit up if you can. Time for your meds." I'm not sure if it's a term of endearment or if she has so many patients that she can't keep their names straight. Turnover is pretty high in the hospice world.

Stacy always smells like stale cigarettes covered up with Clinique Happy. I'm not sure her patients can smell anymore, but I can. It's comforting to me somehow, this cloud of life and sweetness. It's not lost on me that I find that same smell cheap and nauseating when it's coming from DK—Dana. Maybe she isn't so bad.

Glenn comes after work three days a week and for a few hours most Saturdays. He sits with mom and tells her she can get better. That anything is possible. He brings articles he's read and sometimes some holistic cures he has found. It's touching to watch but also heartbreaking to see this man who thinks he has all the answers have none that matter.

Glenn brings in bags of organic groceries and cooks Mom the most tasteless healthy meals. I know they're disgusting because she never eats them. I do. Sam does. What we can choke down. Neither of us has a taste for cardboard.

It happens so gradually that I'm not afraid, watching my mother die. The routine of caring for her, sitting with her as she grows increasingly quieter over the days and months. It's like heating up the water on a frog in a pot. They don't jump out because the heat comes so slowly.

One day, like any other day, the boiling point is reached. The frog is cooked.

The boiling point is one of those rare days when it's just me at the house. I wonder if she waited for that. Sam isn't there yet, and Alice has gone to run an errand. Glenn is still at work. My mother is lying on the couch and unexpectedly reaches for my hand. I hold it in mine and for some crazy reason start singing to her. I am no singer. But I remember this song she always loved.

"Bye bye, Miss American pie," I sing to her.

She looks at me but says nothing. She smiles I think.

DANA (aka DK)

Nikki's attention at work definitely slips during the time of her mother's illness. She passes off some of the grunt work, which is fine. She even misses a couple of big red carpets and photoshoots. Also fine. I cover those. It's good for me because it underlines what I already know.

I am done with all of this.

The adoption agency needs to verify that I have the time and capacity for a baby. I consider nannies and day cares. But I want to be the one the baby knows as his or her mother. Full time. That has required a lot of thought, but I now know for sure. Selling the agency will be my ticket to spending time at home and becoming a mom. I work on converting my home office to a nursery. I am careful to pick neutral colors. I don't care if it's a boy or a girl. Only a child of my own. A family!

"Is your husband happy with the color?" The painter says to me one day. He rolls the walls with a tan paint while I stand in the hallway watching him. I am positioning the crib and changing table in my mind.

"He loves it," I respond.

I have no need to tell this guy there is no husband. Although he is super attractive and charming, I decide against flirting with him.

Blake Hoynacki is the one who mentions Nikki as a possible buyer. I still think of her as a junior associate at best, but she does have Axel. She reminds me so much of myself early on. I wasn't ready when Aunty Cathy left it all to me. Being forced to take over changed me. Maybe it will do the same for Nikki. Blake says she stands to inherit enough money from her mother to make the sale feasible, maybe with a little extra from Axel. Not sure if that is ethical of him to tell me, but he says it in a way that at least allows me to see the possibility. Just one option among a litany of options he suggests, but this one seems like a real possibility.

Then her mother dies. And the wheels are in motion.

BLAKE

I check up on Nikki from time to time. Actually, it's not from time to time. I know precisely how many times I have called her and how many weeks are in between calls. Eventually, it's down to only days in between. I tell myself that it probably seems more casual and random to her.

My first call is to check if she contacted the estate attorney I recommended.

Then I check in on her mother. And her.

At some point, it evolves into chatting. I hear all about her escapades at work and her fights with her brother. I tell her about my *Leave It to Beaver* upbringing and the slimy executive criminals I defend now. Nikki does her usual sarcastic banter. I enjoy the volley. She makes me happy, and although I know this is such a sad time in her life, I think I bring her a little light too.

I get her mom's address and send meals and flowers. For her mother but really for Nikki.

One day I can hear the tears in her hello.

"Hey, is this a bad time?" I say.

"It's never a bad time. Or I wouldn't pick up."

There's a long pause, and I think maybe we lost the connection.

"I'm just so scared," she whispers.

"I'm on my way," I say. I hang up.

In all these weeks of phone calls and deliveries, I have never seen her in person. Never asked her to dinner, never stopped by her office.

Even as I planted the seed with Dana that Nikki might be a good candidate to purchase her company, I never stopped by. Never discussed the opportunity with Nikki. I didn't want to drag our conversation back to professional things now that it had turned into something more. I listen to her. And laugh. And somehow chip away at the blandness of my life before her.

When she opens the door to her mother's house, I can feel death seep from the entryway. Not an odor or anything like that. Just a heaviness and calmness. Nikki falls against me, hugging me, and I let myself exhale.

It is a Sunday night.

NIKKI

The business of death is like this giant circus. You have to go in the tent, but no one even tells you the circus is in town until it's happening to you. You vaguely always knew the circus was out there somewhere on the outskirts, but you never thought of going.

You don't like clowns? Doesn't matter.

You have to pay the price of admission and watch them, the trapeze artists, and the whole damn shebang.

Taxes? Yes, death is taxed.

Court? Yes, you have to go through probate court.

There is no time to mourn because you are too busy hustling between lawyers and accountants. The show must go on.

Then there is the actual funeral home business. They charge for everything—and I mean everything. And you're an asshole if you don't agree to purchase the best of the best. It's your mother, for God's sake!

The visitation is the worst part. Glenn and I stand next to the urn full of my mother's ashes, receiving a line of people. He is in a pinstripe suit, of course. Meticulous. I'm wearing the most conservative thing I can pull together from my entertainment business closet. A black pantsuit with a T-shirt. A large photograph of Mom sits on a table next to the urn in an expensive frame provided by the funeral home, at a premium obviously. It is shaded by a huge bouquet from Axel.

Person after person tells us how sorry he or she is, how they knew our mother, and then they move on down the line and fill the pews for the service. Sam is among this sea of people. No one knows his place in her life, so he isn't comfortable standing with Glenn and me. Frankly, we could use another person in this siege of well-wishers and condolence bearers. Julie is mysteriously absent, but I don't push Glenn when he says she can't make it. Other than cards sent via snail mail, she has been missing in action throughout my mother's illness. Perfection isn't as smooth as it seems and is fraught with mysteries unknown to me.

Alice is the worst. I realize that I carried some kind of grudge against her for years for no real reason, but when I see her crushed by my mother's death, I soften a little. She seriously looks a little dead herself. Lost. She hangs on to me in more of an embrace than a hug in the receiving line. Her cries aren't the silent kind you usually hear at funerals but more like whimpers and shrieks of pain. I defrost for her, and I can see that even Glenn feels for Alice. He rubs her back affectionately as I hold on to her.

After the service, we host a catered gathering at my mother's house, Glenn and me. No longer my mother's house now. Ours until the upcoming auction. I'm grateful we included bar service even though Glenn was opposed at first. I assumed I'd need liquid courage. Turns out, I don't take a single drink that day. I don't even take a Xanax. I clutch a bottle of water.

DK, Dana, is there in a black maxi dress. She picks up empty plates and takes out the trash even though I tell her we have people for that. She says she wants to be useful.

I see Sam talking to a priest. I never knew my mother to be religious, so I'm not sure who invited this guy. I approach them and offer Sam a hug. He collapses a little in my arms before breaking loose and introducing me to Father Dexter. I can't tell if this guy knows the real deal between my mother and Sam, but he is lovely. I'm glad Sam has him.

Once the funeral is over, I dig in to all the work assigned to me by my mother. She left a substantial life insurance policy, perks of working in that office all those years, but being the executor of her will turns out to be less something to lord over my brother and more like a pain in my ass.

DK also wants a meeting. *I mean, damn.* If this is about me missing work, my mother just died! Surely even DK could understand that.

I am so wrong.

When she offers to sell me the PR agency, I feel like the circus elephant has just let out a big, loud elephant yell. He stands up on his hind legs and raises his trunk in the air.

Could things get any crazier? But the more Dana talks, the more I can see it. All the things I love about my job and none of the things I hate. No more snide remarks about my comings and goings. No more desk snoops. Forget the things my mother didn't give me in life, all the petty grievances I held on to for way too long. She has given me the ultimate exit gift.

I take it.

***

"You aren't going to believe this shit," I say to Blake on the phone as soon as I leave DK's office.

"Let me guess. Dana wants to sell the company to you," Blake answers.

"So you knew?"

I don't know if I should be upset that he kept this from me or if he only happened to guess correctly. Then I remember seeing them in the car together all that time ago. *Ahh.*

"I had an idea it might happen," he says. "Are you happy?"

And I think he genuinely cares if I am.

He has seen me at my worst and at my best while caring for my mother. I let him see me cry. Snot cry even. And he is still here. I'm starting to think maybe he wants to be.

The circus is full of surprises.

JULIE

The morning I leave on my little sojourn, I don't go far. I drive to Malibu and check into one of those boutique beach hotels. I want to get room service and sit by a pool all day. No big plans. After a day or two though, I realize I'm no better off than when I was sitting at my kitchen table. The ocean breeze is wonderful, but I have spent enough time on the sidelines of my life.

I'm done with that.

I start looking for apartments, browsing Zillow on my phone. I love looking at all the interiors and imagining the different lives I could live in each locale.

I could be dressed in white linen living in a shabby chic Craftsman. I could be barefoot in overalls digging in my garden. At first, I'm just looking in LA. But it's so expensive. I have money saved from the inheritance my grandfather left me years ago, but it won't last forever.

I broaden my search and become fixated on Ferndale. It looks Victorian, like a real-life Hallmark movie village. I imagine sitting in a window seat in my cute little cottage with a good book and a cup of coffee. Finding a job at a bookstore or yarn shop (is that a thing?). Meeting a handsome stranger.

I don't imagine Glenn in this new life. Or at all.

I move to Ferndale with only what I took in the Tumi. I check in to an Airbnb. It's quaint and picturesque in all the ways I fantasized about. It's also down the street from a homeless shelter. I notice a help wanted sign in the window but ignore it at first. Then I follow a handsome stranger through the door one day.

"Can I help you?" he says as I approach the counter.

Motivational quotes line the walls. Cheery quips. They distract from the dirty paint and secondhand furniture that populate the room. The utilitarian decor could not be more different than the Pinterest boards I have romanticized.

The handsome stranger takes off his backpack as he asks me the question.

"Oh, hi," I say. "I'm looking for volunteer opportunities, and I saw that sign. It says you're hiring?"

"Great!" he says, looking at me. "Our cleaning service bailed last week, so if you don't mind rolling up your sleeves, we need someone to chip in there?" I see that he is young. Tattooed. Not the man of my dreams.

"I would love that," I tell him.

He pulls out an iPad and hands it to me. "Let's get all your info."

I sit down with the iPad on a beat-up office chair, input my new address, and start my new life.

Glenn calls me when his mom dies.

"Julie, it's me," he begins.

"Glenn. How are you?" I'm shocked to see his familiar name pop up on my phone. Shocked to hear the voice I once knew as well as my own now sound so strange and foreign.

"Mom died. The funeral is next week," he tells me.

"She died? I'm so sorry, Glenn. I thought you said she could beat it, that she would beat it," I reply. I walk down the street, vacantly looking at shop windows. Going for coffee, before I start my daily shift at the shelter.

"I thought she would." His voice catches.

"I'll come if you want," I say. "If you think that's something you need."

He hesitates. "I don't think so. It's fine if you don't come, maybe even better if you don't."

We end the call and I walk into my favorite cafe. I decide to splurge on donuts for the shelter residents.

GLENN

With both Mom and Julie gone, no one is left to see me as the man of the family. Certainly not my sister. We play the same cat-and-mouse games and fall back into those kid roles we always are with each other.

I show up at Mom's house the Saturday after the funeral. Per our conversations, Nikki and I plan to pack up everything. The door is locked. Nikki's car is in the drive. *What the hell?*

I bang on the door. I call her cell.

"Hey!" Nikki answers, as if she's glad to hear from me.

"Open the door!" I bark at her.

"Nope. You figure it out," she says. I see her wave from an upstairs window.

Payback.

I can't believe Mom left her to handle everything after her death. But if I'm being truthful, Nikki does a great job. I am such a mess figuring out my own life that I don't think I could do it. I guess Mom knew that. Death sense.

Julie moved to Ferndale. She keeps me apprised of her new life via text and email. Hell, I help fund it at first. She still hasn't filed for divorce, so maybe there's hope for us to return to our old life.

The thing is, I don't want to.

I drive over to West Hollywood a couple times a week. Not until after Mom dies. I somehow want to keep up appearances until then. At first it's straight bars, but I eventually visit the gay bars. I make a few friends.

"Hey, is someone sitting here?" a guy says to me at a little brunch spot one Sunday morning.

"No, take the chair," I reply, looking up from my eggs Benedict.

"On second thought, come join us," he says. I look over to see a long table of men and women laughing, sharing food and mimosas.

I grab my plate and move to their table. "Hi, I'm Glenn," I say, extending my hand.

"Ooh, you got the eggs Benedict," an attractive guy exclaims. "Can I try a bite? I knew I should have ordered that!" He stabs a fork onto my plate.

I sit, no longer hiding.

ALLISON

My dad seems to disappear for a while. His visits are no longer every day, which is okay. I can manage on my own. I'm even driving my car at least but still no bike. I can do my own grocery shopping, but Daddy still brings some by. He never shows up empty-handed. He never sits and chats. He rarely calls. I know for a fact that he hasn't been to see Mom in a while. I'm back to visiting her daily, but it feels more like drudgery than ever. And lonelier.

My father's absence feels all too familiar to me, like my ex's slow fade. Oh, I had a boyfriend. For years. I thought we were lifers, but he never moved in. He never proposed. When I think back on it now, I realize how foolish I was to think it would last. We spent most nights together...then suddenly we didn't.

At first he'd say he was busy at work or had an early meeting. Soon we were seeing each other only on the weekends, and eventually he stopped calling. He avoided my calls and texts. After years together, he had done a slow pull of the Band-Aid.

I was left wondering what happened. The years I gave to him, to us, just *poof*—gone. I woke up alone in my house with a job I couldn't even call a career. And then the whole thing happened with my parents, so I moved in with them and poured myself into my mother.

And here I am now. Empty. Alone.

I want to know what has happened to my dad. He seems so sad. Is this a delayed reaction to the avalanche of sorrow surrounding the demise of my mother? Is it something else?

I'm afraid to ask. Afraid to find out that the cause of his misery is somehow me, just as I fear it was with my boyfriend. My ex-boyfriend.

Juno and I watch an Axel Miller movie on TV.

DANA (aka DK)

I love the way the nursery turns out. All beiges and greens with just a tint of yellow. I spend hours rocking in the rocker, dreaming of what is to come. I don't miss the office at all. Or the nicotine. The two are intertwined in my mind—all part of a girl, a woman, I don't know anymore. I even throw out all my work clothes and fall in love with J.Jill. Flowy pants and tops that barely skim my body. So much more comfortable.

Now that Nikki is in charge, I don't look back. I rip off the rearview mirror. She can figure it out. Even if she doesn't, it's not the end of the world. No babies will die.

When the call comes late one afternoon, I race to the hospital. I don't know what to call myself when I check in at the desk, so I say "visitor."

I step onto the elevator and push the button for the maternity ward. I stop at the nursery window. All those beautiful babies.

And one perfect one.

I hold him in my arms. I can't believe I am allowed to bring him home.

He's the man I've been searching for my whole life.

SAM

I tell no one about the loss I feel when Anne dies. Nikki and Glenn know. And Alice. They allow me to mourn with them. That has to be enough. I know Allison sees a change in me, but I can't burden her with my cross. Father Dexter knows Anne was important to me, but I can't tell him the full truth. I don't deserve his support.

I visit Mary for the first time since losing Anne. She stares at me blankly when I enter her room. I take a seat opposite her wheelchair and put my hands on top of hers, in her lap. Hands the same age as mine. Hands I held most of my life, all my adult life.

I tell her everything. Anne. Our love, her death, my sadness. I see a light in Mary, a glimmer in her eyes. Maybe some of her is still in there after all. The confession is for me. I don't want to hurt her. Then she does the most remarkable thing. She squeezes my hand. I search her face for some understanding but see none. I know then that God has released me of my sin—even if the pain remains. I sit with Mary for a long time.

ALICE

When Annie dies, a part of me does too.

I know that sounds crazy. I get how I must look in all of this, crying more than her kids or Sam, sad as he is. I am sure they think I had some kind of obsessive love for Annie.

But that's not it at all.

I wonder who I will take care of now. That's what I miss the most. I am not sure anyone will ever let me care for them the way Annie did. Even before she was sick, Anne let me take charge.

We were neighbors when she first moved to California. She moved two houses down and across the street from me.

"Hi, I'm your neighbor, Alice," I first said to her, standing on her little front porch, holding a basket of wine and cheese as a housewarming gift. "Welcome to the neighborhood."

"Get in here, and let's open that wine!" Anne motioned me inside the house.

We drank the bottle and ate most of the cheese that first night. She was funny and beautiful, and she talked a lot. About her dead husband, her kids, her new boyfriend. She listened to all my advice. She let me cook her dinner. We became friends.

I am lost about what to do with all the time I have on my hands now, with Anne gone. I go to the mall, the library. Sometimes I drive by her house. I try to help her kids, but I know I'm not really needed. Besides, I find being at Anne's house so hard.

One day when leaving there, I decide to stop by an animal shelter. I intend only to hold the puppies and maybe the kittens. Pet them for a few minutes, see if I can donate.

I fall in love with the last puppy I hold. He sinks into the floor and hides from me. He doesn't want to be held, but I force it.

"What's the story with this little guy?" I ask the shelter worker.

"Oh, Bear has been here for a while. He never barks or begs," she tells me.

"I think he may be sad," I respond, holding Bear's little face in my hands.

I take him home.

I can make him happy.

NIKKI

My mother's urn of ashes is in a box on my closet floor. I don't mean for them to be there for so long, but like I said before, there's a lot to do during the death circus. Plus, I'm now in charge of the entire PR agency. I actually show up to work excited every day. I get rid of the child receptionist and the landlines. Everyone comes and goes as needed and works from home when they can. Best of all, I hire Connie to handle Axel. I sense something brewing there. I may need to go back to being his publicist if she becomes his girlfriend.

Dana is a mom now and is totally immersed in motherhood. I never thought she would relinquish the agency to me, even if I was the rightful owner. But that's exactly what happened. I assumed she would hold on to connections and details, but she didn't. I'm hesitant to call when questions come up, so I don't. I let her enjoy the baby and remind myself that the agency is mine.

I take her a present for the baby. A little tracksuit complete with the smallest Nikes you've ever seen. I ring her doorbell and stand there with my gift bag.

She answers in this beautiful tunic and palazzo pants. The outfit looks gorgeous on her.

"I don't want to bother you," I say. "Just want you to have this." I hand her the bag.

"Nikki!" she exclaims quietly. "Please come in." She makes a *shhhhh* motion with her finger to her mouth. "He's sleeping, but I want you to meet him."

She leads me into the nursery. Tan walls with prints of animals in green and yellow hung throughout. A mobile circles above the crib playing "Entrance of the Gladiators." I peer over the crib railing and see the sweetest little guy swaddled in a blanket and sleeping soundly.

"His name is Knight. Like in shining armor," Dana whispers in awe.

I hug her.

***

Glenn and I pack up Mom's house on the weekends. It takes some time. I find little pieces of her in all kinds of places. Photos of her and Sam. Her and several different men actually, but mainly Sam. She found the one finally.

"I'm not sure what to do with these," Glenn says one day as the Sam photo pile grows.

"Sam should have them," I say. "This is the Anne he knew." I hold up a photo of them at the beach—this hunched-over old man in a sixties-era Hawaiian shirt and long shorts and my mother in a beautiful floral cover-up, holding hands.

Not a lot of our childhoods is left in the house. It's like that part of my mother's life had been put away long ago to make room for the woman she became in the end. I'm not saying we were erased or anything like that. I have most of my childhood stuff, the things I care about anyway. The rest was thrown out long ago. Same for Glenn. The lasting impression I have of my mother is the way she lived moving forward and not dwelling in the past. She bore the loss of my father as best she could by living.

Also my mother was human. She loved and lost and loved again.

She moved on when she needed to and held on to few reminders. I am grateful I came to know her in those last months of her life—and now, in this time with her things after her death. The woman I thought I knew is gone forever, but the woman she really was lives on with me. The bearded lady is a beautiful woman when you get to know her.

Alice wants to help with everything. I find her on the guest room floor one day, holding one of my mother's shirts.

"You can have that if you want," I tell her.

"No. I would never wear it," she chokes out. "Someone should have it who needs it."

The woman is so emotional. Even over a stupid T-shirt.

"Hey, Alice. You've been awesome. But Glenn and I can handle it from here. You don't need to come back," I say. And hearing how that probably sounds, I add, "Of course, you're always welcome. But we don't need any more help."

I know I still sound like the little brat she knows I am.

She leaves that day and goes to an animal shelter. She rescues a puppy. She is so full of leftover love for my mother that she has to put it somewhere. It's sad but also amazing when you think about it. She names the puppy Annie.

Just kidding. Wouldn't that be some shit?

I see this internet ad for death charms. Smartphones know when you're in the market for things like that. Always listening, they know when to send you ads for Tide and when to send you ads for death memorabilia. Anyway, the charms are lockets where you can put the deceased's ashes and then wear them as a necklace or a brooch. I find it morbid, but you know who would appreciate it?

It only takes a few days for the pendant to arrive. I stare at my mother's box in the closet and think, *How do I scoop her out? The same measuring cup I use for baking?* I finally settle on a shot glass. I scoop out about half a shot's worth of Anne and sprinkle it into the locket.

Some of my mother spills on the closet floor. *Do I dust bust that?* I'm afraid to try to put it back in the box for fear of mixing my dust bunnies in with my mother's soul. I finally decide to wipe her up with a tissue and flush her. I stand at the toilet and watch the tiny portion of Anne disappear. I wonder if I should say something churchy.

I go back to the locket and close it up. I finger the engraved *A* on the outside, for Anne. Also for Alice.

I haven't forgotten the slap at the hospital that day. But also, I kind of see that I deserved it.

The alarm goes off at 6:00 a.m., my new wakeup time. I stand in my dark kitchen gulping green juice and supplements, careful not to wake Blake. I load the back of my SUV just as the air starts turning warmer and the day sets in. Another day of sunshine.

It is not a long drive. I find a spot right out front and ring the doorbell as my watch turns over to 6:30.

Allison opens the door.

"Nikki?" she says. She is still in pajamas but drinking coffee and, more importantly, standing up straight and mobile.

"I got you something," I say. I point to my SUV and the two new bikes I've carefully unloaded from it.

"Let's go for a ride."

THE END

Made in the USA
Columbia, SC
27 March 2025